Willesden Herald
New Short Stories 12

Willesden Herald Books

Published simultaneously in the United States
and the United Kingdom in 2022
by Pretend Genius Press

Editor: Stephen Moran
Cover design: Stratos Fountoulis

ISBN 979-8-9859089-1-6

Willesden Herald

New Short Stories 12

Editor: Stephen Moran

www.newshortstories.com

Contents

Introduction

The problem is not that there is too much bad writing out there. That's just the way it is and always has been. To create from nothing, something that matters, no matter how fleetingly, is a difficult trick, impossible for many. To create something that matters from such untrustworthy, mercurial, shifty-eyed bastardy things such as words, well, you get what's coming to you, frankly. And in case you're new to writing: what's coming is usually disappointment, often abject disconsolation. So, there will always be a sea of bad, or even worse, mediocre writing. Like midges at a skinny dip, as unfortunate as inevitable.

No, that is not the problem, not really. The problem we face here is that there is just too damn much good writing, and for those who are paying attention it's driving them to write even better. It's an arms race of narrative technique and invention and it's a tribulation for a hack like myself.

This book you hold in your hands or feet, who am I to judge, is evidence of the robust state of the short story form. On the next pages you will live the lives of an unfortunate baron, Irishmen down on their luck, a young man getting a haircut, an odd nun and many others. Beyond the wide breadth of experiences, their stories are told in a spectrum of styles and voices. What a beautiful thing to read!

Choosing which stories were to be included was difficult. It's apples vs oranges every time. But it had to be done because I don't make the rules. The Willesden Herald does and, like a person under any other brutal autocratic regime, I was only following orders lest they send the goons round.

The only thing that was simple was choosing the winner. From the very first lines *Hotline* by Zakia Uddin announced itself as a story you needed to pay attention to. Each subsequent sentence never disappointed. It was quickly obvious that I was reading the work of a fine craftsman as I was brought to a world that I would never be able to visit outside of fiction. The young London girl away from home with an odd aunt and the charismatic young man. As with the best short stories, it delivers a surprise that is not a surprise. The tension and sensuality of the story is masterful. And that's just one story! *Vevey* by Catherine McNamara is stylistically dense and in contrast to many of the other stories. It has a European feel in style as well as subject matter. The interweaving of time is tricky to do well but here is an exemplar. It's a story full of strange, but effective, use of language to condense a life, a whole family saga, into a few pages. *Cuckquean* by Jackie Morris demonstrates the deft movement through a narrative, knowing when to speed up, slow down, jump cut, etc. The story manages to capture the psychology of the characters perfectly in rich scenes of an everyday tragedy until it drops you off at the gut punch of an ending. I'm grateful that the ranking stopped there and I can just say read these wonderful wonderful stories. They were an absolute pleasure to read and I hope you too will enjoy these writers as much as I did.

Jarred McGinnis
Marseille, 2022

David Butler

Shoes

'You my friend are a life-saver.'

'Hunh,' grunted Burke. The obdurate thunk-thunk had all his attention. It ricocheted like gunshot, rattled again and again the heater's cavernous metal belly. Twice, a pale blue sprite had unfurled over the gauze, gurgled tentatively, vanished. 'Come on, you hape of fuckin…'

Thunk!

From the dilapidated armchair Fagan splayed the toes of a waxen foot, dabbed between them with the tea-towel he'd been handed. Then, between palms, he attempted to impress warmth into their numbness. 'You are one *absolute* life-saver.'

Thunk! This time it caught. The gauze reddened. As though by conjuration the bedsit grew sweet with the odour of long-spent gases.

'Cosy little place you have all the same.' Fagan interrogated the interior for the precise adjective. 'What the Germans call *gemütlich,*' he nodded, satisfied.

'This dump?' Burke looked doubtfully about the basement. His eye took in the sofa-bed, the breeze-block walls, the sink, the one-armed armchair where the other was hunched over an ugly foot, picking at dead white skin. 'How much would you say I shell out for this particular…luxury suite?'

'Wouldn't have a clue, brother.'

'Go on, try.' He stared hard at his lank-haired visitor folded stork-like into the chair, too minutely preoccupied to look up. 'Item: A hotplate. Item: what they call a heating element, if you could call that kid's pencil an element. And you've seen for yourself the bring-your-own-jacks-roll jacks top of the stairs - shared I might add between six of us.' No response, beyond a companionable sniff. 'Have a guess, I'm curious.'

The silence lengthened until Fagan became aware

of it and looked up, eyes unexpectedly naïve in the weather-coarsened face. 'Honestly. Wouldn't have the first clue.' Burke maintained the probing stare. 'Dunno, mate.' Sniff. 'A grand?'

'And the rest of it!'

'*That's* what I was saying to you, brother...'

Unimpressed, Burke lifted the guest's boots, dropped them ostentatiously in front of the heater. They were repulsive to the touch, cold, water-bloated. 'Dry these out for you, anyhow.'

Fagan glanced up momentarily from the task in hand. 'Them lads? They're not worth a fiddler's fuck. Split soles, see? Take in more bloody water than they keep out.' He unfolded his gangling leg toward the gas, wiggled the naked toes. He then pulled on the second thick wool sock Burke had dug out for him. 'Now that's *gemütlich* and all. Telling you, two toasty feet is the Oxford English definition of luxury.' He watched the toes inside each sock alternately clench and unclench. 'Apologies for the display of trench-foot there, yeah? It's a professional hazard.'

Professional, thought Burke.

'Know what I seen once? Up inside of a shop window, for everyone to gawk at. In Amsterdam, it was.'

'Hoors?'

Fagan guffawed. 'That and all! No. What they had,' he framed a rectangle with his hands, 'this huge big glass tank. Filled with tiny fishes it was. You sit up there with your bare feet stuck inside, in full view of everyone. Let the fishes nibble away the dead skin.'

'Did you go for it?'

'You mad? You wouldn't catch me letting anything chaw on my feet. Not anything living anyhow.'

Silence, not yet comfortable, was descending with

the dusk. To break it, Burke rinsed and filled a mug from a stuttering tap. 'You'll have a cuppa? Before…' The preposition hung clumsily between them. Fagan allowed it linger like a midge. 'Go on, so.'

Burke waved the heating element derisorily. 'Seen one of these fellas on your travels? Yer man won't let any of us have an honest to God kettle. On account of the damp, *mar dhea*. I wouldn't mind but he then has the cheek to charge a flat rate for the electric, the mean bloody tyke.' While the mug heated, he swept the clothes off the sofa-bed and flopped inertly onto it. A flail of rain lashed the window. It was a prompt of sorts. 'What size you take, Fagan? Nines?'

'The feet?' Fagan examined them. 'Ten. I think ten. Last I looked.' He nodded towards the sodden boots. 'Them yokes is tens.'

'Would nines do you, but? Only I might be able to dig you out a pair would at least be watertight.' Without leaving the sofa but leaning awkwardly on an elbow, Burke began to rummage in a large cardboard box to one side. Outside, a neon streetlight flickered on, casting the curtain's mesh about the bedsit. After a time, a brogue was waved aloft.

'Mr Burke, you're a ledge.' And when its match came hurtling across the floor, 'You are one absolute fuckin legend.'

There was something agitating Fintan Burke, but if Fagan was aware, he didn't let on. Instead, he was making a comic show of buffing the shoes on a sleeve before trying them. Burke fidgeted, readjusted his posture. 'So the brother's is no go?'

'Told you, I'm what they term *persona non grata.*' The naïve eyes again met Burke's. 'I'll drop around there later, collect my stuff. Then that's me done with them.' His eyes dropped back to the task of testing the brogues. 'Like I say, it's not Frank so much. It's herself.'

'How long are you stopping there now?'

'Well that's it. It'll be four, no, five. Five weeks this Friday. So I get their point.'

'Has she actually said anything?'

'Not in so many words. What I mean, she has. Kind of. She's forever implying. The cold shoulder, know what I'm saying? The stubborn silence. I'm tip-toing on eggshells any time Franky's at work. Hence tramping the streets.' An open palm; blue eyes round and candid as a child's. 'I mean, I get it. It's their gaff. Especially now she's expecting.'

'Look. Was up to me…' Burke began. He wasn't sure how to finish, it seemed. He leaned back, inhaled, raked the fringe back from his forehead. 'Was up to me,' he pressed his eye-sockets with the balls of his palms, rubbed slow circles. 'I'd have no problem you kipping here. You know that.'

'Sure look-it.'

'Yah.' He opened his eyes wide, blinked hard. 'Ach, you know yourself how it is.' He slapped both thighs as though something had been decided between them, and in one movement he was on his feet. 'What d'you take? Sugar?'

'One. No cow juice.'

'Just as well, says you. D'you see a fridge? I'm only sorry I haven't a drop of the pure to liven it up for you.' He handed him the mug, watched Fagan cradle it. He hovered over the armchair. 'If it was up to me. You do know that, Tommy? Yeah?' He flicked a thumb toward the ceiling. 'Only, our friend upstairs…'

'You said.'

'A tight-fisted oul bollox.' He smiled crookedly. 'From Cavan.'

'Sure there you have it.'

Another wild flail of rain rattled the windowpane. 'Are hostels really as bad as all that? A dirty night like this, like.'

'The thing is, not being originally from here.'

'But your passport's Irish, no?'

'Fuck, yeah!'

'Well then?'

'I'm not from *here*, but.' With both thumbs down Fagan gestured the floor. 'Dublin, like.'

'I don't get that.'

'It's what I was trying to explain to you. They do it by county council. Anytime you call them up to ask is there a bed going, that's the first thing they ask.'

'Is that even legal?'

'Oh it's legal, alright. This is Ireland, baby.'

'No wonder there's so many tents sprouting up about the place.'

'Let me tell you something about tents my friend.' Was it a trick of the twilit interior that Fagan's face was now taut as a skull? 'You remember your one was sitting beside me under the ATM? Name of Alie. Glasgow, originally. She's one tough old bird, I'll tell you that. Anyhow, she has this tent, up by Portobello Bridge. So you know you hear these stories about drunken gobshites taken a hilarious slash on the homeless? It's not all urban myth, brother. So this one night, just last Saturday it was, she wakes to hear this liquid drumming down the fly-sheet. Here we fuckin go again, she's thinking — I can't do the accent - and she fires outside all set to go absolute ape-shit at whoever's pissing against her tent, never mind that there's three of them. Only it's not piss. It's lighter fluid.'

'Jesus Christ!'

'Yah.'

'C'mere, did they spark it?'

'That's not the point. Point is, they could have. And herself asleep inside of it.'

Another silence, aspirated only by the gas. All at once the evening resounded with the bells of St Mary's. It drew Burke to the window, where he stood freckled by shadow raindrops. His voice, when it came, was wearier. 'Would you never think of going back down home?'

Did he imagine the disdain in the pause? 'You were me, would you?'

'Point taken.' He turned back from the window, energised. 'Are them shoes any use to you? Try them out, there.'

Tommy Fagan levered himself jerkily out of the chair, a lanky scarecrow in a greatcoat. He clacked the heels smartly, tipped forward and backward, splayed his feet, then executed a Charlie Chaplin waddle about the floor. 'They're the real deal, alright.'

'Take them!'

'You're sure?'

'I haven't worn them, not since the Da's funeral.'

'Yeah I was real sorry to hear that. If I'd of known…'

'Sure how could you have known?'

Silence squatted in the basement interior. It was ended when the Superser gurgled throatily, flapping its flame-flag wildly as it guttered out. 'Perfect!' growled Burke. Already, the cold seemed to be invading the room. 'Well that's fucking A, that is.'

It was Fagan's turn to cross to the window. 'Looks like she's easing off a bit. Guess I better make a move if I'm to collect my gear from the brother's.'

'Yeah?' Burke drummed his fingers noisily on the metal gas heater. 'Have you much to collect?'

'Pfff! Couple of changes of clothes, is all. A few

books. I'll see if Franky has the loan of a knapsack I can borrow till I figure out what I'm doing.' He rocked back and forth on the brogues. 'Thanks for these, man. And the socks, yeah? Them rags I had was literally falling apart on me. Speaking of, you may bin the lot of them after I'm gone, and good fucking riddance.'

'Look, Tommy. Would you not stay on a few days more with Frank, at least until the weather clears? Herself'd hardly put a dog out on a night like tonight.'

'And then what? See what I'm saying?' A smile or a grimace, it was hard to tell in the dusk. 'This country, there's always going to be another cold front moving in off the Atlantic. That's why I'd to get the fuck out in the first place.'

'Yeah but, all the same...' Momentarily, his eyes welled. 'You're braver than me, you know that? You always were, even in school. I often think if I wasn't such a fucking... scared to death of being out there, night like this. That's what it comes down to. Without a dry corner to..., or...or a place to wash, or even do your business, you know?' He looked about the bedsit in desperation. 'Not that I've...'

Burke took a deep, unsteady breath. 'Place I had before this gaff, I was literally on the point of being thrown out. Six weeks' notice they gave. Six. And I could find *nowhere*. I swear to you, I never in my life experienced dread like that. It was there the whole time gnawing at you, last thing at night, first thing when you woke. Winter coming on like the city was baring its teeth. I literally got this place with two nights to spare.'

Fagan shrugged, his hands pushed deeper into the pockets of his greatcoat. 'Thanks for the cuppa, yeah? I better...' he jerked his forehead toward the door.

'Look, Tommy, I'll tell you. You can stash your stuff here if you want. Long as you want, yeah? Only you can't stop here. I swear to God, if it was up to…,' his voice caught. What came out was a plea of kinds. 'Your man upstairs…'

Fagan winked. 'You told me.' But he was im-mobile, as if waiting for something. Some finality. Suddenly Burke was overwhelmed with anger. 'Know what I've been doing, this last ten years? While you've been… Will I tell you? Hard *fucking* graft, that's what. Rain, hail or snow, like everyone else in this glorified anthill. See I've been hauling my arse out of bed every freezing morning at fucking…*stupid* o'clock, in one dead-end shit-hole after another that still ends up swallowing the best half of my take-home. You think that's fun? I'm literally nailed all day to a desk in an open-plan, staring at figures on a computer-screen till my mind is turned to mush. Ten years, Tommy. Ten. That's a fucking lifetime. Coz they don't come back. And for what? For *this*? You imagine I *planned* to end up wearing third-rate suits out of Burton's summer sale?

'Think I didn't have dreams? You know I did. You were there, fuck sake! Instead of which… I've missed, (what?). Maybe three days' work? Like, ever. And one of those for the old man's funeral. So don't you fuckin… Don't you dare tell me…showing up in Dublin after ten years swanning around Europe. And now you're meant to be back? With your communist manifesto and, and your fucked up family and your *world owes me a living*, yeah? Coz I'm not interested, pal…'

As rapidly as it had surged the anger was spent.

'Jesus, dude. Where did that come from?'

Burke stared, appalled. Then he gathered himself, shook his head rigidly from side to side, pronounced each syllable separately, 'I can't. Let you. Crash here. End of.'

'I know, man.'

'Look, Tommy.' He swallowed. 'Stay with Frank.'

'Can't do it, mate.'

'Please. I'm asking you.' He looked at the ceiling, fists clenched. 'He's your brother, Christ's sake.' Tommy Fagan was eyeing him, ironic, amused. 'Just a couple more nights, till the weather clears. What difference can it make?'

'It's decided, man. Told you, I'm well out of it.'

A howl, upward. 'Just ask him, fuck sake!' The vehemence shocked them both.

Fagan guffawed. 'Fintan, Fintan.' He shook his head, made for the door, opened it. 'I'll see you round, brother. Thanks for the shoes, yeah?'

And he was gone.

The room was dark, but for the amber light spilling in from the street, spattering ghost raindrops over walls and furniture. Burke stood a long time, staring at two indistinct shapes that crouched toad-like in the gloom before the dead heater.

'Just ask him,' he repeated. 'Just ask him fuck sake, Tommy.'

Helen Harjak

Remembering not Forgetting

On the day of Pavel Vasilevich Tolstoi's funeral, Nadezda wakes early. She has dreamed of Pavel's mother—her former neighbor Mila. In the dream, Nadezda is in the middle of the lake when Mila calls out to her. She tries to turn the boat around, back toward the shore, but the oars won't budge. Then, a door slams, the elevator creaks into action and somewhere outside a car alarm wails incessantly.

Nadezda eases herself out of bed. She doesn't like to dwell on the past. Over her many years, life has shown that it's safer not to remember. Behind the curtains, darkness still looms, so it must be no more than six in the morning. She stomps her feet a couple of times to get the blood flowing and makes her way to the living room where she's laid out her clothes.

She came upon the funeral notice in the paper by chance. Pavel was still a young man—only in his eighties. She repeated the name several times, letting each syllable sit on her tongue. But she became certain of his identity when she found Mila's own funeral notice between the pages of her old notebook.

Now, Nadezda takes the notebook to the kitchen table and opens it on a blank page. It has been a while since she has thought about the words the village wise woman bestowed upon her. She must have them ready today, arranged in the right order. Her pen hovering over the blank page, she takes stock of her memories.

What does she remember? She remembers she hasn't always lived in this inhospitable city. She was born in a little village by Lake Pskov, in what is now the Pechorsky District of the Russian Federation, just beyond the Estonian border. It all used to be part of the great empire back then. But progress happened: two world wars, with the Revolution and the Independence War in between. Nadezda remembers leaving the village and crossing the lakes in the rowing boat Mila had found. And now? Now, she's an old woman, alone. Even the cats—Rybka, Polina, Kotik—are dead.

But the words? She recalls a dim kitchen, the scent of boiled nettles with something rancid underneath, a rough-hewn table with burns and markings all over. She was nineteen, and Igor had been home from the war for a few weeks. She remembers looking down at her stained apron and wondering why the so-called wise woman had summoned her. Known simply as Lena, this woman was so ingrained in the fabric of the village that it felt like she'd always been there. There were rumors she had helped everyone's great-grandmothers give birth to everyone's grandmothers, although it could have been one of those questionable stories people liked to tell. Lena's wrinkled face squinted at her. "You have strength," her thin lips said, "but I shall give you more."

Nadezda shakes her head at the shy girl sitting at that long-rotten table and worrying about her no-good husband's supper. "What a young fool you were," she tells herself.

She first made a feeble attempt at passing on the words at Mila's funeral eleven years ago. Like Pavel's, Nadezda found the funeral notice by chance. But it was more of a surprise, as she hadn't seen Mila for seventy-odd years, nor known that her friend had made her way to Tallinn. Initially, Nadezda wasn't even sure whether this was the right person. While a Ludmila Nikiforovna born in 1898 had been her neighbor, she didn't understand the addition of this new surname—Tolstaia. The villagers never had third names, although Nadezda had to pick one for herself when she arrived in the city. So, she went to the funeral and was taken aback to recognize a stiff and shriveled Mila in the coffin.

At the burial, a large man she now thinks was Pavel had taken charge, keeping his womenfolk in order like a grieving cockerel. Nadezda expressed her condolences to a bosomy young woman with curly hair, who confirmed that her grandmother had indeed come from a village near Lake Pskov. At some point in the 1920s, the new Estonian authorities had insisted that all descendants of serfs pick themselves a last name, and her grandfather had obliged by choosing this writerly one. The woman told Nadezda she had never been to the village.

"We're in a different country now, Auntie. The village is in Russia, but we're in Estonia," she explained and sighed as if this inconvenienced her. "It was her heart. It runs in the family. But she did well to make it this far—" she fanned herself with her hand, "I'm already worried about mine, and I'm barely thirty. I get these palpitations, you see."

It was at this point that Nadezda thought of the words Lena had given her. She had no children of her own, so why not offer them to Mila's kin? But her explanation must have been garbled as the young woman frowned and excused herself from the conversation soon afterward. She ignored Nadezda for the rest of the afternoon.

This time, Nadezda wants to be prepared. But, as the tip of her pen makes circles above the paper, the words do not come. There's a rhythm to them she can still hum, yet like a long-forgotten song, they remain obscured.

"That won't do," she says and dials the number of the clinic.

*

"That was really not necessary," the doctor tells Nadezda as he takes the box of assorted chocolates and places them on the side. She finds a certain dismissiveness in his gesture. They are past the Best Before date on the box, but he couldn't have made that out so quickly.

"Thank you again for seeing me at such short notice," she says, placing her hand on her heart.

He leans back in his seat and crosses his legs. "Well, we had a cancellation. What seems to be the trouble?"

"I'm worried," Nadezda says, "I'm getting tired easily. I can't remember things."

The doctor glances at the papers in front of him. He takes her blood pressure and shines a bright light into each of her eyes. His fingers are icy despite the rubber gloves he pulls on to poke at her. Nadezda complies, loosening her limbs like a rag doll to follow his demands.

"What day is it? What year is it? What did you have for breakfast?" he asks.

"It's Thursday, September 25, 2003." She checks her wristwatch. "The time is just gone half past ten. And I always have porridge."

The doctor grins, but she cuts him off. "You don't understand. The other day I forgot my Rybka had died…"

"I'm sorry for your loss," he says, staring at her funeral outfit, "Was Rybka a close family member?"

A shadow passes over his face as he realizes. "I see."

"He was a good cat," Nadezda says, "But it's not only him. I'm worried I'm beginning to forget very important things. Like this woman back in my village—"

"Everyone forgets some things." The doctor

drums his pen against the table. "It's a cause for concern if you can't remember what happened yesterday, or an hour ago. As to decades… To tell you the truth, I don't remember much of my youth either."

She stares at his largely unlined face, a bit of grey at the temples, the teeth still gleaming white.

"As for the tiredness, have you taken that iron supplement you were recommended?" he says. "From my point of view, you're doing well. All the tests I can see from your past visits have attested to that. Do you know how many pills most people have to take? For their blood pressure, heart, thyroid, blood, stomach, liver…" He counts them off his fingers. "You, however, have a little bit of understandable weakness for someone in their eighties."

"I'm a bit older than that," Nadezda says. "It seems like it has been an entire century."

The doctor looks down at his file and frowns. "This can't be correct here? You were born in 1901?"

It's not her real birth year, but it's also none of the doctor's business.

"You must be on some sort of register." The doctor riffles through the pages in front of him. "We should have been alerted… I mean, it hasn't been flagged."

"What register?" Nadezda's heart flails in her chest.

"You know, the presidential register. They go and congratulate people who have reached such a… venerable age on TV."

"I don't want to be on TV," she says. This is how it begins: they take your information, then you're on the file.

"Of course, if you don't like that sort of thing, you don't have to," the doctor says, "Do you have much family left? Children?"

She shakes her head. She might as well be honest. "You know, I worry sometimes that my time will never come."

"You're worried about… not dying?" The doctor scratches his chin.

"I think perhaps I might be unable to. You see, we had this wise woman in our village—a sort of a healer, they said."

The doctor's eyebrows move higher, driving lines across his forehead.

"I know what you're thinking, young man: *she must be a deranged old woman*. But this wise woman gave me these words for keeping. And now I'm worried because I can no longer remember what they were." Nadezda feels a flutter underneath her ribs.

The doctor smiles. "There's always time for dying. You, you can still live a little. For your age, you are in magnificent shape. There's a lot we can learn from you actually…" He looks up at the large clock above the door. "I'm afraid our time is up for now. But do get in touch if anything else troubles you. I suggest regular check-ups. I will leave a note for the nurse to call and remind you."

*

At the bus shelter, Nadezda observes other old people and wonders how many pills they take. But no— she already has too much to think about. Without the words, she might as well skip the funeral and walk home. Yet, something is keeping her rooted at the stop. Was dreaming about Mila simply her anxiety over the funeral or a good omen?

To get to the church, she has to change buses, inhale two different sets of humid air, a whiff of petroleum and a lingering combination of stale sweat and alcohol. She hasn't set foot in a church for years, although she assures herself it's more out of lack of need for a ceremony than a superstition.

There was a church in her village, named after Saint Ilya. It burned down the year she became Igor's wife, the same year the Great War started. While many people ran toward the fire, either with pails of water from the lake or simply to gawk at it, she and Igor walked to the tip of the peninsula where they could see the flames' flickering red reflected on the water's dark surface. They stood side by side, and Igor, still looking like the rosy-cheeked boy who had always taunted her at the village swing, said something about fate calling to him, his grey eyes taking on a darker sheen.

She suffered those years he was away fighting for the Tsar's army. Her parents were gone by then, her siblings scattered here and there, and her mother-in-law regarded her as the paupers' daughter who didn't have the decency to produce offspring despite her son's superior seed. When Igor was discharged, he came back a different man. He spent most of his time in the tavern, only acknowledging her existence after a day of drinking, every touch of his now a smack. They were constructing a new church for the village by then, but she never saw the inside. She recalls a ghostly outline receding from view as she pushed down on the oars.

She adjusts her maroon headscarf after getting off the second bus. She likes wearing it tied underneath her chin even when tradition doesn't require it. The two boys from the flat below hers shout *Baba Yaga* every time they see her. Perhaps she is becoming witch-like in her old age? She chuckles as she makes her way to the small wooden church tucked away in the residential neighborhood. As her cautious steps take her across the suburban sidewalk slick with brown leaves at various stages of decay, she's surprised to remember the way so well from the time of Mila's funeral.

Everyone has already moved inside the church. The air is filled with the sweet smell of incense from the censer and the priest leads a chant that makes Nadezda's skin prickle. She stays close to the entrance, letting her glance slide across the mourners. When she came here for Mila's funeral, the church was packed. Now, there are gaps between people. Much easier to see—but also easier to stand out. While she could explain the connection from the village, she doesn't like to encourage useless natter. Beyond the coffin and the mourners, the icon frames and candle stands gleam in the light pouring in from stained-glass windows.

When the time comes to approach the coffin, a curly-haired bosomy woman assumes the role Nadezda had once observed the man in the coffin to hold. It's likely the same woman she spoke to more than a decade ago, although her hair is red rather than blond and her face is swollen from crying. Nadezda's attention is soon drawn to the family by her side at the coffin—a middle-aged couple, trailed by three smaller figures. The woman's face is blotchy and similar to the curly-haired one, even though she's slimmer. The man keeps adjusting his tie with alarming frequency. There are two little boys. But the teenage girl… She is a real beauty, with round green eyes, high cheekbones, and a small, sharp nose. The longer Nadezda considers her, the more she recognizes that the girl resembles young Mila. With their face paint and oddly shorn hair, few young people look this beautiful these days. The girl's parents, the curly-haired woman, Pavel in the coffin—none of them have the same features. At best, she can perhaps make out Vasili's square jawline and tall forehead on the women and the deceased. Vasili was not a bad man, not like Igor. But Nadezda always thought Mila could have had her pick from further afield, made herself a life in the city, become a lady.

Nadezda sees the girl's lively eyes dart back and forth, perhaps searching for another of her kind in this pond of people closer to their deaths than their births. She wonders if the girl has ever been to a church like this before. She doesn't recall seeing any children at Mila's funeral, but then there were an awful lot of people. When Nadezda locks eyes with the girl, she struggles to avert her gaze. It would be the prudent thing to do, but the girl looking at her is really Mila staring back at her across the decades. *Why didn't you write to me*, she seems to say. *Were you angry? Did you find me selfish?*

The girl turns away first, but something in Nadezda's memory has dislodged. As the priest takes up his chant again, the words the wise woman whispered at her scarred kitchen table come back to her. First, one by one, then, line by line—like a song that once again snakes its way through Nadezda's mind.

*

In the summer of 1917, a few nights after the wise woman had summoned her, Nadezda was making supper. She had memorized the words to appease Lena, but she hadn't repeated them again like she'd been instructed. A part of her still wondered if the old woman would somehow know she hadn't done it and send for her again. When she had left Lena's house, she'd noticed a woman with a knock-kneed child waiting outside. She could accept that Lena was a healer with herbs and potions. But she doubted she could magically straighten these legs. And she couldn't be immortal either—no matter what the villagers whispered.

In the lazy August heat, a film of sweat had formed on Nadezda's upper lip. She leaned out of the window to get some fresh air as the smell of cabbage and boiled bones started to turn her stomach. No use—there was a ripeness to the air outside as well. She looked at the horizon, birds in a V-like formation over the lake. Going south already? There came a sudden hiss behind her, the soup overboiling even though she had kept the fire low. She used a rag to soak up some of it and burned her thumb. As she held it, a thunderclap drew her attention back to the window. The yellowed curtain was flapping in the breeze, although there had been no wind a moment ago. A wave of heat seemed to travel through her. Nadezda sat down and put her head in her hands. A mild patter told her it had started to rain. She didn't think she stayed there for long. But when she looked up, the room had grown darker and Igor stood there, his face red and eyes wild.

"I see we have a lady of leisure here. How is your day, Madam?" The stench of vodka reached her in wafts, like exclamation points at the end of Igor's sentences. There was always a fool or two at the tavern who would buy a drink for the "suffering veteran", as he was in the habit of describing himself. Nadezda usually knew how to handle him but still avoided letting him catch her off guard.

Igor moved to the stove and stuck his hand in the pot. "What is this raw, cold shit you're making me eat? Is this what I fought for?"

She tried to get up, but the liquid was flying everywhere, with the pot stopping just short of her toes. The metal ladle caught on her arm.

"I hear all you're doing all day is going to see that old witch," Igor hissed.

"She invited me." Nadezda sighed, thinking she couldn't as much as cross a road without one of Igor's kin witnessing it.

"No doubt to poison me. I know what you women are like. You think I'm stupid, don't you? You think I'm a fool, while you can act like a queen? Well, guess what—being married to a fool doesn't make you a queen."

Igor's laughter was long and hollow as he let himself sink onto a chair. She remained standing, too cautious to move. He put his elbows on the table and leaned his forehead on his arms.

"I'm sorry," she said and reached out a hand that was promptly batted away. He was up again, yet she was moving too, running toward the back room. If she managed to close the door before he got there, he would go into the kitchen, perhaps light his pipe and calm down. But the edge of the rug caught her foot. As she tried to shut the door, Igor's sinewy arm made it through, and he applied all his weight to open it. She backed away, clutching at the splintery edge of the bedframe. He launched into a speech that touched on her failure to give him a son, on the difference between men and women, and the parable of the fox and wolf, where the fox abandons the wolf when his tail gets frozen in ice. Nadezda closed her eyes and repeated the words Lena had given her.

*

Despite being one of the first to leave the church, Nadezda is late to the burial, arriving just as the priest finishes his blessing. Most people must have driven here, while she was stuck on the bus, which went in an unexpected direction due to some diversion or other. A few people glance up as Nadezda approaches the grave, trying to keep her footsteps light. She half-meets their eyes and nods politely. A balding man inclines his head, while the curly-haired woman from the church starts whispering something to someone whose face is hidden under an enormous felt hat. Nadezda averts her gaze and moves toward the back of the crowd where she extracts an embroidered handkerchief and pats her nose with it. She senses someone's eyes on her. The pretty teenage girl is looking at her again. Nadezda gives her a nod, and the girl turns away quickly.

When Pavel is in the ground and the lush wreaths of lilies and chrysanthemums are arranged on the fresh mound, the mourners gather for photographs. Nadezda lets people crowd in front of her. As the photographer gradually whittles down the group to teary-eyed close family only, a few people walk off, while others start taking out food and drink. Nadezda restrains her surprise at this departure from tradition—who is she to judge, after all—and edges further into the general commotion. Before she can refuse, somebody has handed her a shot of vodka. She clutches the bit of liquid in a plastic cup, politely declining the offer of a boiled egg and a piece of black bread by another person. When she spots the teenager's father standing to the side and observing the activity around him, she holds out her cup. "Perhaps, you need it more than I do?" she says.

The man shakes his head and takes the cup. "But it's getting colder. You may need it yourself."

"My old bones are used to the cold."

She notices the three children huddled around the slim woman with the blotchy face. The taller of the little boys looks like he might be in primary school, while the smallest is still a toddler.

"Are these your children?" Nadezda asks.

"Yes! I'm sorry. I'm Jaan, and this is my wife, Marina. And the children." The man waves in their direction and sips the contents of the cup.

"Move along then," the woman says to the children before turning to Nadezda. The teenage girl walks away, followed by her small brothers.

"I couldn't decide whether it would be a good idea to bring the young ones," Marina says. "You want them to have that culture... But then they get bored and disturb everyone."

"Oh, it's nice to see young people here," Nadezda says. "Otherwise, I'll think that we're all so very old and there's no future."

"So how did you know my uncle?"

Nadezda senses Marina studying her face. "I knew Pavel's mother, Ludmila. From back in the village."

"You knew grandma Lusya!" Marina's eyes seem to come alive. "Were you at her funeral? In 1992? I don't remember seeing you."

"We'd lost touch for many years, but I wanted to come say goodbye," Nadezda says, "I didn't stay for long." She's conscious of the curly-haired woman somewhere nearby.

"Of course, there were a lot of people then," Marina says. "Many more than now. I was still a young mother. So young!" She runs her fingers through her feathered brownish-red hair. "Teresa was only little."

"Teresa is your oldest?"

Marina nods, but her attention seems to be hijacked by the fact that someone's topping up her husband's plastic cup with more vodka. Nadezda uses this diversion to edge away as she pretends to read the messages on wreaths. She spots the children a little further, all standing still and looking at some bushes. After a quick glance back to make sure nobody's paying attention, she takes the pine needle-strewn path. They don't notice her until she's only a few meters from them.

"What are you doing, children?" she asks.

"Nothing!" comes the quick response from the older boy.

"We saw a kitty, aunty," says the toddler.

The brothers clamber after the cat. Teresa tells them not to go too far before turning to Nadezda. "Who are you again?"

Nadezda smiles. The girl is clearly sharp.

"In the village where your great-grandmother Ludmila was from, there lived a wise woman called Lena," she says.

"I don't remember my great-grandmother."

"Doesn't matter," says Nadezda. "This woman, Lena, helped people. You could say she was a healer."

"Like a witch?" Teresa raises an eyebrow.

Nadezda nods. "You could say that. She had some powerful words."

Teresa leans her head to one side. With a strained smile, she says, "I'm not a baby. If it's just a scary story, you might have better luck with them." She points toward her brothers who are now a few plots down.

"What I have to say is not for babies," says Nadezda, "babies wouldn't know what to do with it."

"OK," the girl says and glances at the graveside gathering.

"When I was about your age… Well, a little older, I guess—for I was already married—we used to get married a lot younger back then. Your great-grandmother did as well. She was a real beauty. Just like you, Teresa."

The girl furrows her brow. "How do you know my name?"

Nadezda looks over her shoulder at the funeral party that is getting livelier. "Your parents... That doesn't matter."

"Did my parents put you up to this? Is it about the time I went to that party with Karolina?"

"I don't know any Karolina." Nadezda would like to move toward the closest tree trunk and lean against it, but she's worried the girl would take it as her cue to walk away. She wonders if her waning strength is a sign to leave the girl alone. Yet the words are bubbling up in her mind, as if impatient to be spoken aloud.

"This wise woman..." Nadezda says. "I was called to her house. What she told me that afternoon, what she taught me—she was a very old woman, mind—maybe older than I'm now—she taught me the words to see me through hardship. She said I was already strong, that this kind of power can only be given to one with a strong constitution."

She takes a few unsteady steps toward the tree and smiles at the girl. "I'm not so strong anymore."

"Are you OK?" Teresa moves closer. "I can ask my parents..."

"No, no, I'll be fine," Nadezda says. "Are you strong, Teresa?"

The girl shakes her head. "I don't know."

"You're looking after your brothers."

"Well... My mum is sad about Uncle Pavel."

Nadezda nods and says, "That wise woman told me she could heal many illnesses. But she also had another kind of power."

The girl crosses her arms over her chest and peers at Nadezda. "Are you saying she had magical powers?"

"You can call it whatever you like. What Lena gave me were potent words."

Teresa's eyes hesitate, yet there's still a twist of

amusement to her lips.

"Girl, I need you to take this seriously," Nadezda says, "I'm about one hundred and five now and my memory isn't always reliable. But when I saw you at the church today…"

Teresa shakes her head, serious now. "Nobody's that old! That would mean what…"—she narrows her eyes— "…you were born in the nineteenth century?"

"Something like that, yes," Nadezda says. "I had to change my papers. My husband… He wasn't a good man anymore. I had to leave." She touches the smooth skin of the girl's arm. Teresa shifts from foot to foot but doesn't shake herself from her grip.

"What did you do then?" she asks.

"I came here," Nadezda says. "It wasn't easy. It was still wartime. I could tell nobody wanted me here. But that's how life was back then—we survived."

She thinks of being on the lake for days, the hesitation she felt when deciding which way to go. She resolved to stay away from the eye of the revolution in Petrograd. Everyone she met told her she was going in the wrong direction. The Germans were coming. But when the Germans arrived, she kept her head down. No, that was much later—a different war. The Germans didn't get far the first time. Nadezda's heart quivers. "Don't be afraid," she says. She no longer knows if it's meant for the girl or for herself, but the girl nods, her eyes studying Nadezda the same way Mila observed her on her last day in the village.

"Those words," Nadezda says. "They will serve you. They will keep you safe and alive for as long as you wish. And when you're ready, you can pass them on—like I'm passing them on to you."

Teresa widens her eyes. "Why me?"

"I think our Mila led me here to you." Nadezda

wants to take the handkerchief and dry the tears from the corners of her eyes, but she doesn't want to let go of the girl. "Will you take them?" she asks.

"How does that even work?" Teresa says.

Nadezda feels her shoulders relax. "Now, here's what you need to do."

*

Nadezda dreamed of a band of beautiful women dancing around her bed. They scattered pink and purple daisies on her and braided her hair. They sprayed a sweet scent on her body and whispered prayers over her. She wanted to get up and tell them they'd made a mistake, that she wasn't dead. But she was afraid of upsetting them as they were trying to make her look nice. She thought if she breathed out heavily enough, they would make the discovery for themselves.

"Easy there," said Mila, leaning over Nadezda, a hand on her chest. "It's alright, you're alright." She put a pillow behind Nadezda's back, helping her sit up. Nadezda looked around, noting she was in the bedroom she shared with Igor.

"Igor," she said.

"Bastard!" Mila sighed. "I'm glad they locked him up this time. He was running along the main road screaming like a madman."

Nadezda nodded and sipped from the cup of water offered to her.

"You are safe for now," Mila said. "Though, of course, he'll be out again soon."

Nadezda started to cry. At least she thought these were tears—her face was wet.

Mila wiped the corners of her eyes. "You weren't moving at all when I found you on the floor," she said.

Nadezda made to get up. She remembered saying

the words now, the unbelieving look on Igor's face.

"Are you sure you're alright?" Mila asked. "Who knows what injuries you may have?"

Nadezda stood up and stretched. There was no pain in the places where Igor's blows usually landed.

"I'm worried about you," Mila said.

Nadezda shook her head. "I'm fine. It's all fine."

Mila looked at a spot on the floor. "Igor has been saying things about you," she said. "That you've put some witchcraft on him, that maybe you've been doing it for a while."

Nadezda laughed but stopped when she saw her friend's sober glance. "You know that's not true. That's just the way he is now: babbling nonsense after a drink too many."

Mila shook her head and came over to Nadezda. "The things he's saying about you—it doesn't make any sense, of course. But some people... his family might believe him."

"What are you talking about?"

"This morning, I thought I would go to that old witch to see if she would back you up, say that she has not helped you curse your husband. But when I got near her house, there was all this commotion. Everyone standing around chattering as if they had nothing better to do! Lev the Drunk was there, holding a half-empty bottle. I was about to say, 'Lev, the sun's not even high yet, what are you drinking that beer for?' when Lev said, 'The old crone has disappeared.' He wiped his nose on his sleeve—disgusting man—and said, 'It's probably the new church that did it, chased the old devil away.'"

Mila's cheeks glowed as she searched for something in Nadezda's face. "Perhaps," she said after a pause, "it's safer for you to go as well."

"Go where?"

"You always said you wanted to see a city."

"How would I manage on my own?"

"There are jobs—I've heard they take on women at factories now. Or maybe you can be some rich lady's maid, like the story we read at school?"

The thought of being out there in the world was taking the breath out of Nadezda's chest. Igor had gone there and see what happened to him.

Nadezda swallowed and took Mila's hands in hers. "I'll go if you come with me."

Mila smiled but pulled her hands away and went back to the bed. She adjusted the pillow and smoothed the blanket. "A boat," she said, turning to face Nadezda again. "There are all sorts on the roads now. They say you can row all the way north into Lake Peipus. Vasili knows men who go fishing there."

"We can take turns rowing," Nadezda said.

"I'll try to get us a boat," Mila said. "You gather what you need for the journey."

After she left, Nadezda paced around the room wondering about Lena. Perhaps she had to urgently visit a relative in another village who had taken ill? But why had she called on Nadezda and given her this strange spell? If Lena intended for Nadezda to somehow take over from her as a wise woman, she had said nothing of the sort. More likely, she had failed to help someone in need and was now in hiding. Nadezda needed to have her wits about her. "Leave the phantom-chasing and lamentations to the likes of Igor," she told herself.

By the time Mila returned, Nadezda had dug through the rags in the mattress and uncovered a couple of paper notes and silver coins. Mila said she'd found a boat and would go and see to her own affairs. Nadezda waited until nightfall before going to their meeting spot.

The moon—a waxing crescent—was partly clouded, but she still managed to find the boat between the reeds. Squinting into the darkness, she thought she saw someone and held her breath wishing it to be Mila. Further along, she could just make out the white walls of the new church. As the moving figure came closer, Nadezda was relieved to recognize her friend's gait. But there was also a heaviness to the way Mila walked, as if she hadn't packed light the way she'd advised Nadezda to do. When Mila finally appeared in front of her, she wasn't carrying any sack.

"You didn't bring anything," Nadezda said. A lump in her chest was gathering weight like a snowball. Unable to make out Mila's expression in the dark, Nadezda waited for her to say something. Had she come to believe Igor's ravings?

"I think you better be on your way." Mila moved closer, coming to kneel in the shallow water by the boat. Tears covered her face. "I'm sorry, my dear Nadia. I don't think I can leave Vasili."

Nadezda hugged her friend and shed tears as well, though anger squeezed her heart.

*

Nadezda shudders when the girl pulls her hand away. Daylight is beginning to fade.

"I need to get my brothers," Teresa says.

"Do you remember what you need to do when you get home?"

The girl repeats the words like a poem she's been made to learn by heart, a little too earnestly, mispronouncing a word here and there as if saying them out loud renders them devoid of meaning.

"Thank you," says Nadezda.

Teresa shrugs and heads down one of the narrow

paths between the graves. Nadezda walks away too, turning right before Pavel's grave to avoid saying goodbye to anyone else.

On the bus again, after staring at a young man to give up the closest aisle seat, Nadezda wonders whether Teresa believed her and if she will go through with it. Had Lena also wondered? And what were these words for, really? Nadezda just lived her meagre life. Working at the plywood factory in the city was difficult, but she had never known idleness. And she loved Dmitri, his sparkling eyes and lopsided mouth, the way he stood up at meetings and the way he used to tilt his head when he listened to what she had to say. One day—it must have been in the middle of the 1920s—he didn't come home. She asked around among the trusted comrades and found out there had been a raid at a meeting. There was a list of those arrested, but his name wasn't on it. She knew she'd be in trouble if she went to the authorities, so she went home and waited. He never returned to her. Later, when the next war started, she heard a rumor of him being in some unit or other. The Germans came and all the comrades disappeared. Only later did she recognize some names and faces again, call up some old acquaintances for favors. She loved the flat in the new-built block she was given after decades of dingy rooms and shared kitchens. Then, the times changed again, and now her area is undesirable, a mixture of lonely old people and angry young men in tracksuits. But it's only in early spring or midsummer when she sometimes craves the village, to be away from these concrete walls and touch the cool water of the lake or smell the honeyed scent of lindens in the grove.

When she gets off the bus, she notices it has grown warmer outside. Underneath her woolen coat, her dress sticks to her back. A gentle breeze rustles up some leaves and chocolate wrappers that saunter down the sidewalk by her feet. A young man with a scarf tied around his neck walks past. Surely, it's too warm for the scarf? She almost says it out loud, but the man seems already to be talking to someone. Is he a madman conversing with himself, she wonders, or does he have one of those telephones everyone is mumbling into these days?

She has started to feel sprightlier. The wind in her face is warm and smells of sunnier days. Yet there's a certain ripeness to it—probably from all the rotten leaves gathering underneath the trees. She unties her headscarf, lets it flutter in the breeze. She would like to walk a little more, but the sun is going down and it's no hour for an old woman to be pottering around by herself. She doesn't even check whether the elevator is working, deciding to take the stairs. As she makes her climb, nausea creeps over her. It's a smell of some sort. No more of ripeness but another kind of stench. Cabbage, it comes to her. She hasn't eaten cabbage soup for decades, all the meals she cooked for Igor best forgotten. She swallows hard, hoping she won't vomit here and now. It would be embarrassing if any of the neighbors happen to walk past or look out of their peepholes. Yes, she's an old lady and they will take pity on her. But she doesn't need their pity.

She hastens up the last set of stairs, unlocking her front door with trembling hands. Without stopping to extract the keys from the lock, she rushes to open her living room window. The air still smells warm and ripe—she hasn't been imagining it. There! A flock of birds forms a perfect V. It's the right time of year, she thinks. Before the thunderclap, before the rain starts falling, she remembers everything.

Catherine McNamara

Vevey

Ada's fiancé was a fighter pilot from Tel Aviv who died before her eyes in a long arm of smoke not far from the tarmac. She remembered the walk to the wreck, taking off her heels and the weight of Georgie's wet arm. Yves had had one green eye, one grey, and made young Ada choose a colour each time they made love. Grey would command and injure, green would spiral into her essences and claw these apart.

Five years after Yves's death Ada married Pierre who had indifferent greasy hair and wore glasses that were thick reflecting discs. Pierre was Swiss and liked the Ivorian girls who came into his office. But at fifty-nine Pierre had a fatal heart seizure in Grande Bassam and a woman was seen hurriedly catching a taxi in the street. After the funeral, Ada's dry-eyed sons – a doctor and a cellist – flew back to the States. For Ada had elected to move in with her younger sister Georgie who lived in the mountains north of Lake Geneva. Long ago, ignoring Ada's fraudulent advice, Georgie had married a tall German with a polio limp and borne him three flawless daughters.

Ada is in Vevey, it is her last day at the apartment. A homeless Moroccan Jew with thirty-three boxes, she sits waiting for the removalists' truck. Her dead husband Pierre's boxes are to the right. They aren't going any further than the local cast-off shop. If Ada were to stay here on the Lake she might easily have seen one of his African shirts on a pleased man. But it is definitive now, everything has been sold off. In his casket Pierre looked as though he had just relished a good fondue, instead he had embroiled their savings in an Abidjan hotel complex that had washed into the sea.

The removal people ring to say half the office has come down with a spring flu and the secretary has a coughing fit which ends the call. Ada is left holding the earpiece. She rings her sister Georgie, but Georgie's limping German husband answers with his unconditionally loving voice, and she is reminded that her three radiant nieces came from a firmament of love, unlike her own sons who were the spoils of lamplit sex. Ada puts down the phone and cries. In a week she will be sitting on a wooden bench halfway to pinnacles wearing Georgie's trousers, with glimpses of his stagger between sheds.

If Yves had not fallen out of the sky her life would never have followed its zigzagging path between Treichville and Vevey, between riotous West Africa and leaf-strewn Europe. Yves would have taken her back to Rabat and given her a daughter. Yves would have built a stone house with alcoves for succulents. To Yves's funeral they had let Ada lead the convoy up the hill, a drenched posy in her hands and everything through the gauze of her veil. Georgie trod next to her with glossy, black eyes. Ada was just twenty; it should have been the day of Ada's wedding.

Five years later Pierre saw Ada's trained thighs dancing in Fez and pulled her down in his room when he was a coaxing man just free of his rudimentary family. Her sons were born in shattering, red-faced succession. As they grew, Ada smoked behind the bamboo screen in the corner of the patio, watching these sons cocooned on a pair of breastless, barefoot house-girls' backs.

Ada peers down to the Lake through the neglected ray of opaque window panes and knows that soon enough another woman's sharp-eyed cleaner will be up on a stool with veins behind her knees. There is no food left in the cupboards, nought but the last swab of coffee powder and a sandcastle of cane sugar in a bowl.

She has kept enough just for this morning, thinking of bulky men requiring orders, and keeping these men alert. She knows that later, when the removalists are gone and her belongings are all on their fractured, immaterial paths to nowhere, her face will be a sobbing mess. She will drag her mauve suitcase onto the landing and listen to the last clench of her front doors. Ada knows at this point she will place her palms on the sage green panels and these panels will refute her touch.

She feels her bowels flutter. She ought to buy a bottle of red wine as it seems she will have to sleep a further night here on the mattress she has earmarked for the Carmelites.

Ada leaves the building. Down on the promenade she casts her eyes back to the apartment's gay window sashes and sees their imminent betrayal. Who could say that ownership is more than a fable? What has she owned any more than the reeking man at the train station with criss-crossed palms? She pictures the boxes choking her hall, the resumé of her marriage in a plump man filling a casket, and a failed appointment with a removalists' truck. She thinks of all the *stuff* she has harboured these years, and how the thing she has guarded most has been the short-lived choice between Yves's unequal eyes. The dazzling afternoon bursts over Ada's shoulders and thick hair. In the distance she sees the spine of blue mountains where her sister lives like a motionless dead end, the place where she will certainly lose her mind. She refuses any contemplation of the nutty air and preposterous dimensions. She gets Georgie on the line this time and tells her there would be no need to come down this afternoon.

Ada walks or glides within the garment of her body with its channels of involuntary purpose. Her distant abdomen swills. She releases a warm *pfft*. Her long-untouched nipples are crimped within her brassiere and the fingers that now sweep her face are not her own, they surely belong to a woman with cold, unused blood. Out on the Lake a girl turns a sailing boat and Ada remembers her vivid knuckles on varnished wood. She watches the girl push away the boom, the hull swivels and wind punches out the sail, sweeping the craft on a straight line into the waves. The removal people finally have the decency to answer and a different, unconvincing speaker tells her she will have to wait till the end of the week. Ada gasps. This is when Ada envisages some sort of bivouacking in the apartment rather than slipping into a hotel, given the buyers may as well have paid in buttons. Ada and Pierre had become so bogged in the sediment of their lives that they were friendless.

Now lightheaded, angry and unconcerned, she walks into the train station and buys a baguette sandwich with tuna, sits down pretending to wait for a train until the long packet is empty and she brushes crumbs from her camel pants. A criss-crossed palm is extended to her and Ada sees it is the station's vagrant. This man's unguarded eyes traces Pierre's apologetic gold pendant dropping between her breasts, and she notices for the first time with compulsion that one of his eyes is grey, the other a stimulated green.

Ada asks the man his name. He replies that it is Terrence.

The two eyes unify upon her.

Ada's spine straightens against the bricks and her face tilts into the path of that dirty visage. Sensations of entrapment are revived. As she stares into the vagrant's mismatched eyes an ancient oscillation, truncated and charred as her fiancé Yves's remains, swings through her like a monkey in a cage.

'Terrence. I apologise for staring,' Ada says. 'You have such eyes – '

These two planets have drifted to Ada's handbag on the bench. She notes another woman giving her warning looks. But Ada peers back through him. Her eyes scout his body which is a lean concentrate of baggy, belted denim. Ruddy skin reaches down his neck, his face is a field of prickles. *Could this man be a messenger, some tributary of her fiancé's effacement?* Ada's eyes take in the rough palm thrust towards her, the overturned wrist with its collar of dirt. She feels an ugly urge to lay her cheek upon it.

At the apartment, Pierre's lifeless clothes lie ironed in five boxes in her hall. There are winter coats, buttoned blazers, collections of Liberty ties and silk scarves, reams of trousers, cashmere sweaters she had stored each time her husband's projects detained him in hotel suites through the tropics. Ada tries to picture this rank man washed and combed and wearing one of her husband's African shirts. Or trying on Pierre's loafers with a pair of clean white socks. Rapture and dismay surge in her body as her bladder burns and Yves's scorched body plunges once more to the salted earth.

'Terrence,' she says, feeling the wall pressed to her back. 'Terrence, my husband has passed away and I have a lot of old clothing at my house. Why don't you come with me and see if there's something you might find useful?'

Ada knows that her sister Georgie – already concerned – would have her head on a plate. But had they not hobbled to the wreck, Georgie shielding her from the licking flames and the black nub of his head, the ash falling, falling?

*

Ada returns to the café awning outside the station and buys another tuna baguette sandwich and two cans of beer. The girl bobs under the counter looking for a carrier bag. Ada marks time, staring at a floodlit incline of overlapping pastries. She turns around to see Terrence's palm held out to a man with his hand in a pocket. The man extracts coins that are enclosed by Terrence's fist.

Ada pays and snatches the bag. She marches out of the train station with half a mind to jettison it in the nearest bin. What on earth is she was doing? She knows there are no charitable reaches in her soul, a dozen years in West Africa had cured her of that. She searches for deterrents while hurrying towards the promenade, where white scrolls tumble over the blue bed of the lake. She peers into a jewellery shop, the scent of her own breath meandering over her face, just as the vagrant ambles around the corner and continues after her. Ada crosses to the generous furs in a glossy window as the bag twists on her arm. She peruses.

In front of her cherished opera theatre with fresh posters for La Traviata, Ada is swept aside by a young striding woman. This woman whips past her with a vital perfume as though Ada has ceased to exist.

Ada reaches the promenade, where she raises her eyes to Georgie's mountains at the end of the body of water with their current admonition and years of altitude ahead. Further along, she sees the vagrant staring at gulls like a boy.

'Terrence?'

He has a thickly-articulated walk, his face fallen and arms muscling the air as though he is in flight from a low threat. She sees he is uneasy with the openness; he has not followed her here to give volume to his thoughts. He suddenly bends at the waist to rifle through a rubbish bin, finding an old sandwich. Ada half-shrieks as he raises it to his mouth. He seems unaware of her and the flapping carrier bag.

She calls him again and his eyes spring to her. But he does not walk any closer. He consumes the sandwich. He rubs his brown face, puts a hand in his denim pocket, his hair a stiff, rank blond already tossing in the wind. His expression turns to deal with her, so that Ada worries he thinks she is to blame for whatever strands of his tragedy are now running loose. Clutching her pendant, she knows she is disliked. He tears away from her face to assess the components surrounding her, the ring of sumptuous apartments including her own ex-residence, while Ada feels like imploring him, begging the frontiers of his eyes, explaining her clouded worth. *I am a good person, you know. I have lived a good life.* She bows away and her eyes cast out over the lake. Full-bellied sailing boats tilt over and she spots the glazed afternoon ferry, the stained light in massive mountains atop the mountains themselves.

'Well,' she says. 'Here, then. Terrence.'

She marches over and hands him the carrier bag and Terrence pulls out a fresh sandwich which he unwraps fiercely. She hears the paper tearing and his teeth plunging through bread, the intimate entry of food into his body. Her phone buzzes and she knows it is her sister Georgie, checking up on the aftermath of the removalists. She ignores the phone and lets Georgie stomp off to her husband's reflective embrace and her configurations of sheep. Hair flies over her face. She listens to his famished mastication and the beer can cracked open and she cannot ward off her distaste for replenishment. In all these years her now-defunct husband Pierre had only grown broader, fattened by his ravenous life. Even the disposal of his dead body had required gusto and phenomenal hand-outs, and when his accounts had come to light she'd had a week-long migraine of throwing up her insides.

Her fingers tighten around the apartment keys in her handbag, which she'd been told by a grinning youth to deposit at the agency. Terrence finally stops slurping from the can. She isn't sure she is able to look unwaveringly at him, with this negligible distance and her pulsating wish to stare. She does not know if she is able to address Yves's resurrected eyes which might be devastating markers dragging her down to their lost, isolated terrain. Her shoulders are stricken. She imagines Terrence's hands around her neck.

'Thank you,' the vagrant says. He tosses his refuse into the water. Her arms sail up in fury then collapse at her sides.

The man has spoken to her. She does not reply, uncertain if he is being facetious and the two words belong to a deviant design. She sees his fist that is almost a bursting fruit with its tan throttled colour. Terrence takes a few steps towards the shore where the water cuffs up and runs back into itself. He doesn't trust the waves, she can see, wondering if his tragedies have their origins there. She looks at his rumpled back. The man stands against the lake and the landscape seems to envelope him while stirring his fears, absorbing him with the sickly afterglow of a Symbolist painting. There is a current running through him, or perhaps it is his noiseless scream ringing on the air. It seems that the waves are declaring, *We shall bear you, we shall bear you.* She is certain she can hear these words beneath their rush.

When he turns around she knows that his arms have once held a drowned child. She looks as far away as she can, for she has been responsible for this afternoon's vast elegy. Terrence wipes his damp face and opens the second can of beer.

*

When their father was killed Ada and her sister Georgie were sent to Marseilles to stay with an aunt. The girls' father had been strict, also an air force pilot, though he was killed by a clean shot to the chest so his body was dressed and calmly beautiful. This was long before Yves, long before the polio-stricken German husband. They were young virgins with ripe skin and velvet black hair that was much admired. It was the summer and they worked in a cousin's restaurant at night, walking home arm in arm after dark, their aunt shouting at them if they should stray out of the quartier.

Their aunt was childless and had never married, she had thick legs that would reluctantly carry her down the stairs and for fatigued stretches along the neighbouring streets. Their aunt was not widely liked, the girls saw, feeling sorry for her. They obeyed her at first – for she was their father's oldest sister – until they too found her bellowing insufferable. Soon enough they agreed to go out with two young men who worked at a nearby restaurant, who took them to narrow dancing bars around the port.

One night their aunt changed the lock on her front door and the girls were forced to sleep at the house of one of the young men. They were uncertain, they huddled together in the kitchen and the young men asked, *What are you afraid of? You can't be afraid of us!* They drank more wine and then some coloured spirits from a bottle on the shelf. Both girls begged to go to sleep. But the boys encouraged them to drink a little more, to finish off the evening, while one of them put on a pot of mint tea. Georgie wandered off to the bathroom to be sick. Ada pushed away the boy who began kissing her. She lay down and fell asleep on a couch, pulling a tablecloth over her dress. In the morning Georgie came out of the bedroom with a wretched crying and marks on her thighs.

They walked home arm-in-arm over the silvery cobbles. Georgie told her how they each took her, the things they pushed into her. She looked along the street steadily, one tender foot in front of the other, her sandals looped on her wrist, her dazed face raw. Back at the house their aunt slapped them both hard on the cheek and they were sent home to their grieving mother in Rabat who also slapped them hard. A month later the aunt died and Ada and Georgie looked at each other in shock, for they knew they had sent her to her grave.

At home there was a horrid 'uncle' who lived upstairs. Ada grew to think that what had happened to Georgie was her fault. To make things align again, she let this man take her virginity with his dog yapping in the next room. She undressed, he fucked her on the bed. Then she went home and showered, thinking about this entry point on her body, on all women's bodies. Sometimes she pushed things into herself, when she was dry and it hurt, so that she felt horror, watching the object see-sawing in and out. She did not tell her sister, but she began to love Georgie more elaborately than she had loved her before.

When she was nineteen they were sent to the kibbutz where she met Yves.

*

Terrence lobs his half-full can into the water and there is nothing Ada can do to stop him. The gulls wheel around, they bother him. Ada realises it is partly because he knows he is prey, he knows that a day will come when he will be outstretched on the ground and they will pluck out his eyes. She can't even guess the last time he sat down at a table. But now her cutlery is packed away, her tablecloths and her pans; any sort of ingredient to work with has been banished from her refrigerator, also earmarked for the nuns. She doesn't even have a bottle of wine to open.

Not that Terrence seem to recall celebration, or be in any need of it. She can smell how the sun has drawn out the clamminess soaked through his clothes and wonders where she might locate some bath towels, and soap. She thinks it could be in one of the boxes by the bathroom door.

'Shall we be off then?' Ada asks him and he seems to nod. She wonders if he is some sort of touchstone who has glided into her life, and wishes that soft, banal questions would drift between them. What has he kept sacred of his past, in the shabby cupboard of his body? How long has he been wandering like a stray dog?

She remembers sighting him years ago on a corner, holding out the criss-crossed hand. She remembers herding her sons away from his stench, never piecing together the details of his face. Her sons had made faces, one had thrust out a tongue.

She wonders about the instalments of Terrence's memory.

She introduces him into her building.

Unlocking the front door of the apartment that is no longer hers, she seizes a form of victory as she strides through warm, echoing rooms. Terrence follows her closely. She still has not turned to meet his eyes. She knows that she will face him at some point, perhaps over the meaningful lake, and pursue gentle investigation of his splintered past. If he will allow her.

They stand at the window, looking down to where

they had been before, when the landscape had absorbed him and she had sensed his torture. She steps into his orbit.

'In some ways we are perhaps as haunted as one another,' she said, and immediately a welt of presumption blazes on her face.

There is no response to be had from him.

'Do you have a family, Terrence? Or did you, once?'

Head-on, she has decided.

He stares out the window. 'This is your house?'

'It is no longer my house, Terrence. It was, until yesterday.'

He frowns at her with a flash of green, a knot of turbulent grey.

'I am going to live in the mountains with my younger sister. We are not close, or not at present. Her husband is a German.'

He has stopped listening.

'Do you have hot water here?'

'Yes, it is still connected. Let me find you what you need.'

Where before she had felt his eyes chafing Pierre's gold chain between her breasts, Terrence's eyes are now unconcerned. They flit across her shoulders, down to her hands, across her forehead, deep behind her. She is in the way of something he is remembering or marshalling into shape.

When she come back his hands are on the glass in broad dirty instruments and she wonders if he had been a musician. The lake is sullied through the blur. She stands watching him poised in the empty room, holding a clean blue towel and a bottle of bath soap. She thinks of Georgie, how it isn't true at all that they are not close, it was just that Georgie hounded her. Georgie is younger and sturdier but she knows her sister will go first and it will be the most brutal event in her life. After Yves. Terrence turns around with the late dusky light pounding behind him and his eyes belong to Yves with the grey so strident, while the green licks around her neck and chin.

She wants to cry, *Your eyes belong to my beloved Yves, and he is gone from me.*

She hears the bathroom door close and the jets turned on. She moves Pierre's boxes under the large hall light and knifes the first one open. Her dead husband's fleshy smell rises from the ironed garments she throws on the floor. Each one she lifts had once contained the body splayed on a bed, a petite lover employed between his thighs. She looks for smaller things. A shirt, sweaters, several impossible pairs of pants; a woven belt from some African boutique. She piles these aside, knowing that none will fit the slim vagrant. She sits back on her haunches listening to the cascading shower. She thinks of the summer of Yves's death: how she had crawled under the wires and laid three days in the dirt where the husk of his aircraft had been and they had never found her; how the sun had burnt her skin so badly Georgie had dressed her for a month but she still bore scars.

Ada hears the shower jets cease. She can hear the water running off his limbs, she hears him release a long, beautiful male sigh. If Terrence will listen, she wants to tell him about Yves's plane tunnelling out of the whiteness, about how he had hurt her and governed her and continued to do so now; and perhaps Terrence in turn will tell her whom he had lost and why he had become a train station beggar holding out his hand.

Terrence paces out of the bathroom naked and he ignores her arms outstretched with Pierre's clothing. He smells like fruit and seems to know his way to her bedroom, where she dimly follows and he opens her shirt and pulls down her brassiere straps, grasping her to his soft skin. They are locked together. There are sounds garbling through her, but she knows she will not speak through these hours. It is too shadowy in here to decipher his eyes and she avoids the furrow between them; mostly she watches his flinty movement over her and sometimes the anchor of his face. There is friction between the dread and bliss of her selves as he arches into her; her efforts go into quelling both of these.

In the night she awakens and he is carved around her exhaling in light, impermanent breaths. This is when she feels the thread of extinction and her arm travels behind, her palm up and down the warm plane of his back.

After dawn she sits up on the mattress, for he is gone.

Early, Ada washes herself over and over. She folds away Pierre's clothes on the floor, she knows he has taken nothing. Her fury returns and she calls the removal people. She swears at the office girl, demanding to speak with her boss. She uses strong language and afterwards, she sees her hands are shaking. She calls Georgie and nearly cries when she hears her sister's voice. Georgie, though distracted, says she would drive down to the city, she just has to find a lost sheep.

Ada stands above the mattress with its new dark maps, falling to her knees to kiss and inhale. She hoists over the dusty prism and it thumps on the floor. Her final cup of coffee she drinks by the grainy window, making lists.

*

A week later Ada is installed at her sister's place in a downstairs room opening onto a brief deck. Her boxes have gone into storage, apart from Pierre's clothing which went directly to the cast-off shop, and the furniture and items she could never keep which went to the nuns. The small wardrobe in her new bedroom has been built and varnished by her accomplished German brother-in-law, who walks with an even more laborious limp nowadays, and who stoops to kiss Georgie's upturned rosy face at least a dozen times a day. Ada's flawless nieces visit one by one from foreign cities where they are studying, each girl a delight.

A month passes and Ada is becoming used to the bold air; her calf and thigh muscles no longer ache. Her bottom has grown harder and her eyes glitter, she sees.

If she thinks of Terrence it is with stained secrecy. She goes back, trying to pinpoint the moment she became complicit. On some days it would be when she felt the pressure of the bricks against her back at the train station, bathed by his eyes. Other times it would be the moment Ada watched him turn away from the water, his arms nursing the drowned child and his silent scream ringing on the air. Sometimes she thinks of Terrence and Yves as one man deep inside of her. She feels the demanding tones of a unique set of eyes: her core wells and she gives herself to their final whimpers, embraces their chill flesh, the act of love a murder.

She will never go to Vevey again.

Her sister, though still immensely occupied with her animals and interests, is in the final throes of domestic momentum. Soon, Georgie will be clutched on a bench with her, surrounded by green turf in the brazen wind. The present will become waxy, and the past would come back like burning sons locked in their wombs. The sisters will bicker, recalling ditties and boyfriends and dresses sewn for them. They will apologise and confess, their hugs watched warmly by the German on a balcony, two ripe young virgins who have not yet loved.

Andy Mead

Haircut

Some things never leave you. The smell of burning wood and plastic always takes me back fifty years. To the burnt black bones of the barber shop, the twisted corrugated iron, the grotesque lump of melted rubber and vinyl, and the two smashed portraits face down on top of each other in the smoking ashes.

The first time I went for a haircut on my own, it was summer. Usually my mother had to drag me to the barbershop. I hated having my haircut and the barber was a miserable old man. The sky was as blue as a baby's blanket and the sun bounced back off the white stone path and hurt your eyes. There was no breeze and no shade. The mango trees were too far back from the fence and the macca bushes had been chopped back to stumps and stuck out of the ground like the spikes of a trap.

It was still only nine o'clock but the main street was packed. Bicycles and mopeds weaved in and out of the cars, trucks, country buses and donkeys. Market day. Saturday, haircut day. I dragged my feet past the Dentist's house, with its twisted iron gate, and yard littered with fallen mangoes. Past the cinema with its Doric columns and garish posters advertising the latest Western triple bill. There was a crowd outside the betting shop, men in working clothes, clutching fists full of pound notes, looking anxiously up at the blackboard where Mikey Blake's cousin Dollar was chalking up the results from some racecourse in England called Kempton. Past the cool dark cave of Mr Lewis's tailor shop, the old man sat behind his ancient black Singer, his half glasses glinting in the gloom.

At last I stood outside Mr Nelson's barbershop. A

square wooden hut on concrete blocks with rickety steps up to the saloon doors. Two scrawny dogs lay in the shade under the shack twitching as they slept, their ribs rising and falling gently. I could hear low voices from inside, I couldn't catch the words.

I sat on the bottom step and looked out across the street. Icy the ice shop man was sliding blocks of ice off the back of a truck. Wrapped in sacking, they disappeared into the cool room while the truck driver sat smoking on a stack of old tyres in the shade of a tamarind tree. Inside the voices were getting louder, the old barber chair squeaking as it turned. It sounded like an argument, but I still couldn't make out what they were saying. I stood up to move closer to the doors when they swung open, slamming back against the wooden walls with a crack. A man came stumbling down the steps, the barber's cape still around his neck and half his face covered with shaving lather. Behind him came Mr Nelson waving a cut-throat razor in one hand and in the other, a blue and white striped towel. The man, who I didn't recognize, ran across the crowded street. Ripping the cape from his neck he dropped it on the bonnet of a black car that braked to avoid hitting him. He shot a mouthful of abuse at the driver and disappeared into the bushes and trees behind the ice shop. Mr Nelson did not follow him. He stood at the top of the steps and roared

'Doan come back inna my shap yu teifin dawg.'

His arms dropped to his side as he looked down at me, kissed his teeth loudly and swore under his breath. A small boy with a huge afro ran up the steps and handed Mr Nelson the cape he had retrieved from the road. Mr Nelson took it from him without a word and jerked his head at me.

'Come,' he said, pushing the swing doors open with

his backside.

I followed, nervously and climbed up into the chair. The shop smelt of hair oil, bay rum and sweat. In one corner was a tin sink and a single swan necked tap which dripped permanently, with a dull ping. In the opposite corner was a low three- legged stool beside a pile of old boxing magazines where Mr Nelson would sit when he had no customers. Beside the big black chair with the chrome base was an ancient tea trolley with a wheel missing, propped up with a couple of old encyclopaedias which looked as though they'd been left out in the rain. On this were Mr Nelson's tools of the trade. Scissors, combs, the razor, tins of pomade jars, of oil and a hand mirror. Plugged into the light socket which hung over the chair were the clippers. But the outstanding feature of this emporium were the two huge portraits which hung on the side walls facing each other. Joe Louis 'The Brown Bomber' and Max Schmeling, the great white hope of Nazi Germany. I didn't know the significance of these two fighters at the time. They were just two boxers, one white one black. All I knew then, was when I was facing Max Schmeling Mr Nelson had only just started and when I was staring at Joe Louis he was nearly finished.

Mr Nelson never said much and today he said even less. He spun me round to face Max Schmeling and his fingers clamped to the top of my head to keep it still. I heard the buzz of the clippers as he started and felt the steel teeth, cold against my scalp. After a couple of minutes there was a shout from outside. He stopped, dropped the clippers onto the tea trolley and picking up the razor he pushed through the doors onto the steps. I froze in the chair. The shouts outside got louder and I could hear the voice of the man who had run away,

'Come awn,' he was shouting, 'come ovah ya mek

me chop yu up.'

Then the shrill voice of a Woman,

'Lard Gad Missa Nelson him ave a cutlass doan go near im,' and a muddle of shouts, voices, screams and the screeching of brakes. I didn't dare go outside. There was a man with a cutlass threatening to cut Mr Nelson up, if Mr Nelson didn't get him with the razor first. Gradually the voices seemed to get further away until all I could hear was the sound of the traffic and the mumbling of voices as people passed on the crowded street. Still I didn't move. I sat staring at Max Schmeling, his dark eyes seemed to be looking right at me, his gloves raised as if to say 'Come on then….yellow belly.'

It was quiet. The traffic in the street murmured and the tin roof cracked in the morning sun. Max Schmeling never moved. The nylon cape was making my neck itch, and sweat was running down into my eyes but for some reason I couldn't move. Something told me I had to wait for Mr Nelson to come back. He'd only just started. I couldn't go with half a haircut. The minutes crawled by. I had no idea how long I'd been sitting there when I heard a heavy tread on the steps and Mr Nelson lumbered into the shop. He was breathing heavily, his face shone with sweat and he appeared to be limping. He threw the razor, onto the trolley, picked up the clippers, swung me round to face Joe Louis and started on the other side of my head. He was muttering swear words under his breath, and grunting as if he was in pain. He pushed my head forward and I was looking down at the floor.

The clippers dug into my neck as he pushed them hard, up and across my scalp, my chin was on my chest so I was looking backwards when I saw the blood.

Around his feet and seeping through the cracks in the polished floorboards. With a groan, he dropped the clippers onto the trolley, pulled the cape from my neck, shook the hair onto the floor and held out his hand for the money. I scrabbled around in my pocket, pulled out two shillings and dropped them into his shaking palm. I looked up at his face, his eyes were closed and he was swaying like he was drunk.

'Yu aaright missa Nelson?' I asked.

'Gwaan bwoy,' he held on to the chair and shook his head, blinking and breathing noisily through his nose. My eyes were drawn to the floor again where the pool of blood was spreading. Still holding tight to the arm of the chair, Mr Nelson took a step forward and pushed me towards the swing doors 'Mi seh gwaan bwoy,' he said again. I ran. Into the mid-morning maelstrom of trucks, cars, bikes and humanity. Reaching the gas station on the corner, I skidded to a stop and looked around. Who should I tell? There was no one at home. Both my parents were out either working or visiting. My brothers never took anything I ever said seriously. Being the youngest I knew nothing and was always, 'a mek up story.' I looked back down the street. Eggy Small was coming towards me with a big grin on his face, carrying a rusty old bike frame and two red mullet strung on a piece of palm leaf. 'Wha appen yute,' he asked. I told him what had just happened and how I didn't know who to tell or what to do. 'Jeezas' he gasped. Yu tink im a go dead?'

'Mi no know man but mi see whole heap a blood.'

'Come,' he said. 'Mi a go a mi uncle yard fi gi im de fish, im wi know wha fi do.'

We set off running across the forecourt dodging taxis and headed down Barrett Street towards the sea. Eggy's uncle, Ras Ronny lived in an amazing house he had built himself out of salvaged timber from a wreck on a sandbank about a mile offshore, pieces of corrugated iron and old enamel advertising signs. It was an amazing looking structure, two storeys connected by a wrought iron spiral staircase he had 'acquired' from who knows where. The upstairs room had a stained-glass window, salvaged from an abandoned Anglican church up in the bush somewhere. He was sitting on a tree stump supping from a chipped white enamel mug when we ran into the yard.

'Whoa whoa whoa,' he called, 'tek it easy. Why oonoo pickney affi move so fas. A duppy yu a run fram?' Eggy sunk to his knees and breathlessly told Ronny the story.

Ras Ronny sat quite still nodding, then looking up at me he asked, 'Yu know dis man wid de cutlass?'

'No sah mi no know im but Missah Nelson run im dung wid im razor an when im come back di razor ave blood pon i blade an im nevah look too good. Mi see whole heap a blood pon i floor.'

'Aaright, aaaright,' said Ronny. 'Come we go dung deh an tek a look.'

Eggy hung the fish up in the outside kitchen, threw the bike frame under the house and we followed Ras Ronny through a maze of alleyways and through scrappy bits of bush till we emerged beside the ice shop. The street was still crowded as we crossed the road, but the barbershop was quiet. I feared the worst. Ras Ronny climbed the steps and stuck his head over the saloon doors. Eggy and I stood nervously behind him. He pushed open the doors and stepped inside. They swung back and hit Eggy in the face as he pushed past me anxious to get in and see the blood. There was no sign of Mr Nelson. Ras Ronny stood beside the chair, picked up the razor and wiped away all the blood while Eggy stared fascinated at the pool of blood on the floor.

'Im gawn,' said Ronny in a low voice. 'Come awn, we haffi fine im.' He had to drag Eggy away from the blood. Once again we trotted along behind Ras Ronny as he led us round to the back of the barbershop through a small stand of guava trees into a yard that was full of old cars, trucks and farm machinery. Some of them were so rusty and smashed up they looked beyond repair it seemed as if someone was trying to restore some of them. The yard smelt of old oil and rubber. In the corner was a small wooden house. It was bright blue, with a red roof. Ras Ronny walked up to the door and knocked loudly.

'Kennet,' he called. 'Kennet yu inside dere.' There was no answer. He tried the door and it swung open. We all pushed inside.

Mr Nelson was sitting in a rocking chair with his head back and his eyes closed. As we got closer he opened his eyes and tried to get up but Ronny eased him back into the chair, pulled another chair from under the dining table and lifted Mr Nelson's leg up to rest on it. Mr Nelson had tied an old bicycle inner tube around the top of his right leg and his trouser leg was ripped to reveal a long, deep cut to his calf. 'A who do dis Kennet?' Ronny asked. Mr Nelson muttered a name that I couldn't quite catch and closed his eyes again. Ras Ronny turned to us.

'Egbert, go fetch you Auntie Bee. Tell ar fi come dung a Maas Kennet yard an carry di medsin bag.' Eggy was standing with his mouth open looking at the gash in Mr Nelson's leg. 'Gwaan bwoy!' snapped Ronny. 'Yu want i man dead?' Eggy grabbed my arm and we ran, all the way back to Ras Ronny's yard. I waited outside while he went in to fetch Auntie Bee. She came out carrying a green canvas bag with strange writing all over it. Her braids were tied up in a bright yellow and orange wrap. She was a tall handsome woman and I'd always been a bit afraid of her. She led the way back to Mr Nelson's yard and told us to stay outside while she went in. Eggy opened the door of the nearest rusty car and sat behind the wheel.

'Di man mussi chap im good,' he said. His eyes were shining and he was obviously excited by the whole gory business. 'Yu tink missa Nelson cut di man wid im razor?'

'A tink im mussa cut im cause mi see blood pon i razor.'

'Im might dead if Missa Nelson cut im up bad,' Eggy said, his eyes eyes wide.

I didn't say anything. I thought again about the first thing Ras Ronny had done in the barbershop. Wiped the blood off the razor! Maybe he had the same idea. If Mr Nelson had killed him, the police would be coming for Mr Nelson. Maybe me and Eggy too.

Ras Ronny appeared at the door and called Eggy. Eggy ran across and Ronny bent down and spoke quietly to him. Eggy looked across at me and nodded and Ronny went back inside.

'Wha im seh to yu?' I asked.

'Im seh we fi go back a de barbershop and fetch di razor. But no mek nobady see wi.'

'Wah im want i razor fa?' I asked, although I had a pretty good idea why.

'Im nevah tell mi. Im jus seh go inna di shop and carry di razor come fi him and doan mek nobaddy see yu.'

I felt a small prickle of fear run down my spine but Eggy's eyes were shining. 'Come,' he said and he set off through the guava trees.

'Hol on!' I shouted after him, 'how yu a go reach inside di shop so nobaddy cyan see yu?'

'Mi cyan go troo de windah a de back but yu will haffe push mi up.' He stopped running.

We both crouched behind the hibiscus bushes in sight of the shop. The window was high up, and small. It had a wooden shutter instead of glass, that lifted upwards and was propped open with a piece of wood. Keeping low we both ran over. I got behind Eggy and pushed him up. He grabbed the sill and pulled himself up and over catching the prop with his foot as he went so it slammed shut behind him. I ran back to the bushes to wait for him. I can't have been back in my hiding place for more than a few seconds before a figure emerged from the bushes to my right carrying a kerosene tin. I went rigid with fear. It was the man with the cutlass. Missa Nelson couldn't have cut him up too badly as he was clearly still very much alive. He crossed to the shop and began to tip the contents of the tin all over the back wall, throwing it around so it splashed everywhere. I could smell the kerosene, I realised what he was doing but was unable to move. He took a box of matches from his pocket struck one and the whole back wall of the shop went up in a sheet of flame. He then turned, flung the kerosene tin so it landed right in front of me and disappeared into the bushes. I could hear shouts from the street as the smoke and flames shot up into the sky.

'Brigade, call di fire brigade!' I ran round to the front of the shop and up the steps.

Eggy was lying on the floor under the window and he wasn't moving.

'Eggy! Git up,' I yelled, 'di place a bun up.'

He still didn't move so I shot across, grabbed his

arm and dragged him out. As he bumped down the steps he came to and started mumbling, 'Di razor mi haffee get di razor.' I dragged him to his feet and ran pulling him stumbling along behind me till we were back in the bushes. I looked back at the shop which by now was engulfed in flames. Eggy was sitting beside me with a huge bump on his forehead still mumbling about the razor.

I thought it would be best if we disappeared pretty quick before somebody thought we had started the fire. Eggy still wasn't quite sure what was going on but by the time we got back to Mr Nelson's yard he had begun to grasp the seriousness of the situation. The flames and smoke were reaching high up into the sky now as Ras Ronny and Auntie Bee came outside to see what was happening. I told the story. Eggy looked at me with wide eyes.

'Yu save mi life,' he said. Ras Ronny smiled and patted me on the head.

'Di two a you betta go home now,' he said. 'Doan seh nuttin to nobady bout dis, yu hear mi? Nuttin at all to nobady. Yu a lissen to me Egbert?' Eggy nodded and looked sideways at me. I knew it would be hard for Eggy. He loved to run his mouth. We both walked to the road at the front of Missa Nelson's house and ran to Eggy's yard where we collapsed under a mango tree.

'If yu talk bout dis an police hear seh me an yu know someting dem wi lock we up.' I panted. Eggy was about to say something, so I kept on talking, 'an if di man wi di machete ketch we im will chop up di two a we.'

Eggy gulped. 'Jeezas God,' he whispered. Doan worry mi nah seh nuttin at all.'

He was true to his word. Neither of us spoke about

that day again except to each other. Missa Nelson's barber shop was cleared away and the plot was soon covered in weeds and bushes. Much to my relief and Eggy's disappointment, Missa Nelson didn't die, but he didn't cut hair again. I was his last customer. Ras Ronny said he was ok just fixing up his old cars and selling them. As for the machete guy, Ronny told us we would never see him again. He said Auntie Bee had dealt with him, whatever that meant. I didn't dare ask. Joe Louis and Max Schmeling, a bit burnt round the edges ended up on the walls of Icy's ice shop. A bit of a contrast to their last home. I still hate having my hair cut.

Jackie Morris

Cuckquean

R eg puts her hand into the pocket of her husband's old coat, snatched up minutes ago to shield her from the chill evening air, and finds—what? Her fingertips, searching for spare chicken pellets, had not expected this silky slippiness.

The chickens fuss over imaginary beetles. Their tiny dinosaur heads wobble in outrage. This is not the way the evening should go: the woman motionless by the run, staring at her hand. It should be the big man who brings wriggly mealworms and kneels to stroke their oh so soft feathers and lifts them into the coop, though they can easily make their own way up, who whispers, 'Goodnight Midnight, Goodnight Sparkle, Goodnight Starlight, Shhh now, Shhh,' and closes the door so they are safe in the darkness.

Reg squints at the whatever-it-is. Her glasses are on the kitchen table. She shakes the material out and finds herself holding a pair of women's pants. Dark blue lace, or maybe black. 'Pants' seems far too prosaic a word for such wispiness. Reg, who has broadened every-where since she hit fifty, no longer frequents the aisles that stock this type of thing.

She sticks one finger through a leg hole and lets the … lingerie … dangle. It's nearly dark, but she doesn't want to bring it inside, though of course that's where it's been, snug and safe in Richard's pocket. For how long? She heads back up the garden, into the yellow rectangle of light cast from the kitchen window.

Perhaps they are a present for her. She holds them as if they were pegged taut on a washing line. They might get halfway up one of her thighs. She raises them to her nose, sniffs. They smell of the sea. A faint silvery trail on the crotch.

Used.

Richard has used, lacy panties in his jacket pocket,

amongst the chicken pellets and the garage receipts and the extra strong mints he likes to take with him on his afternoon walks.

Reg sits on the metal bench outside the back door. Reg and Richard bought this bench from the garden centre when the children were small, to make it easier to take their wellies off. Richard wanted a wooden bench. Is that how it starts? A battle in a garden centre a million years ago somehow leading to used pants in a husband's jacket pocket? Not even a smart jacket, a grimy, earth-stained oilskin. A jacket that's lived quietly on the back of the kitchen door, as if nothing ever happened to it. And all the time it's been privy to … what?

He could have found them. But why would he keep them? That would make him —who—a thief? Voyeur? Pervert? Rapist? Adulterer? When did Richard last wear this jacket? Not last weekend, he was away at some chicken fanciers get together. The weekend before? So many times since he retired he's popped out, grabbed this coat with a cheery 'Won't be long.' So many times she's watched the tall, white-haired streak of him, hands in pockets, stomp down the garden and out of the back gate. So many times she's been quietly pleased to have him out of the house; shaken her head at the scruffiness of him; hoped he wouldn't meet anyone they knew, dressed like that.

How can her Richard have these things? Her Richard, with the slightly hunched shoulders, who looks at her carefully over his wire framed glasses before he speaks. Who sat patiently with Matthew, night after night, as they built Meccano, until Matthew deemed it boring. Who learned all about miniature lop-eared rabbits for Molly and who buried their tiny, flayed carcasses a year later when the fox got into the run. The man she feels spasm inside her every time he comes. Which he still does, albeit not recently, but that, she had thought until now, was to be expected, after all this time.

Darkness creeps up the garden. An owl hoots in the woods beyond the stone wall. The chickens *cluck, cluck, cluck,* spreading the word that Reg is a *cuck-cuck-cuck* quean.

Cuckquean. 'The wife of an adulterous husband.' They hadn't known the word at the pub quiz. Two glasses of wine in, so she'd put her hand on Richard's knee and told him loudly she'd cut his balls off and the whole table had laughed. *As if,* she'd thought. *As if.*

She's never liked the chickens. They are Richard's retirement project: hours spent poring over chicken-keeping websites to pick the right breed: Light Sussex, Dorking, Black Rock, their names reeled out over dinner like some exotic shipping forecast. A three-hour round trip to a specialised breeder to bring them home. More hours down by the coop as he waited for them to lay their first eggs. Six months of single-minded attention.

She'd thought.

Her gut churns. She tastes copper, saliva floods her mouth. She stumbles to the flower bed to vomit and is obscurely proud she didn't make a mess on the path. She can still do some things right.

What now? Go inside, phone Richard. But how can she? Maybe he's with this woman, this owner of lacy bits of cloth that are so easily bundled into pockets, and not at the pub at all. How can she know? Does she want to know?

'Reggie? What are you doing sitting in the dark?'

Here he is, the low, familiar sound of him. The early years of their marriage, she always quickened at the mellow bass of his voice, unexpected from his thin frame. Is this what the skinny, lingerie-wearing other woman likes too? Reg stuffs the pants back into the coat.

'Oh hello,' she says. 'Just thinking.'

'You didn't do the chickens,' he says, with a note of reproach. He heads down to the run and ushers them in, closes the coop door: does all the things Richard always does. It's like sitting in an audience watching an actor you've met in real life.

'Any chance of a cuppa?' he asks as he comes back up the path. He looks tired. Poor Richard. But that's the old way of thinking. He's tired because he's been out fucking. Because whilst she's been here, playing house, he's been out fucking in an alley, or in his car, or up against a tree in the woods.

And the irony of that, she thinks, is it was her who wanted to do all that fucking, and him who said no. Too tired. Got to get up early. Too tired. Until her hand stopped sliding over his back at night and fell between her own legs instead.

She's been tempted once or twice over the years. There was a tennis instructor whose shirt rode up over lean abs when he served. A young, blond waiter at a cafe who looked at Reg in a way that left her jangled. But then she'd think of the big bed only she and Richard had ever slept in. Of how to explain to the children, my god the children, that their mother couldn't keep it in her sensible middle-age pants and she'd tidied those thoughts away, focussed on all she did have, not what was lacking.

In the kitchen, she hangs his coat on the hook whilst he fusses with two mugs and the milk. She's struck by the length of his legs in his battered jeans, the sinews in his arms.

'Do you remember when we met?'

'Of course.' He squeezes the teabag on the side of the mug with the spoon. 'You carved our names on that tree. Bloody terrifying. My first kiss and there I was, tattooed onto a tree with you.' They smile at the same time. It's an old story. He never asked why she owned a penknife, even once they were married, when she slept with it under her pillow. These days she keeps it in the kitchen drawer, a relic to remind her how she snagged Glenister's eldest. The one destined for law school after the holidays. *Spotted Dick*, the lads called him, because of the acne spattered over his face. Spotted Dick, a boy who couldn't believe his luck when the wild girl in the leather biker's jacket went over and asked for a swig from his can. And then a surprise: a delicious, un-expected secret. Once he touched her, she wanted him too.

Back in those days, and here's a bit they never tell the children, Accidents Happened. Especially if you were young and impatient and the condom wasn't on properly. And he was a decent lad, after all, well brought up, and *Oh my god*, he'd muttered when he proposed, his hand on her belly. He knew her background: who didn't? But still: *It'll be ok, Reggie, we'll make it work.*

And they had. She thought they had. She'd given her leather jacket to the charity shop and cried all the way home on the bus, twisting the small diamond ring round her finger. She'd taken out her nose stud. She'd made sure dinner was on the table. She'd bitten her tongue again and again: nearly off sometimes. She'd done everything he wanted. Hadn't she?

Richard puts her mug of tea on the table. She grabs his hand. The calluses on his fingers from his years at the lumberyard are still there, they haven't softened yet.

She kisses the palm of his hand once, twice, and reaches up on tiptoes to kiss his lips: full-tongued, urgent. A kiss to remind him. To remind her.

He sleeps immediately afterwards. His eyelashes flutter now and then. Is he dreaming of Reg? Or some young, impossibly nubile woman splayed out in sexy underwear? Reg doesn't sleep. She doesn't sleep and doesn't sleep and doesn't sleep and doesn't sleep until light seeps through the chinks between the curtains they've had since the children were babies.

In the grey morning light, Richard half wakes, mutters. Reg's chest aches like she's been kicked and bruises are forming. Richard breathes deeply, turns on his side. He's always had a hairy back. She stared at it often enough, pushed herself against it late at night for comfort. She knows his back is not objectively beautiful, but she used to think it was. This morning, it's just an old man's hairy back.

It's cold in the kitchen. Her mug from last night sits on the table where they left it. She fumbles in Richard's jacket and pulls out the pants - navy blue, it turns out, with a tiny red rosebud embroidered in the middle. Cheap. Flimsy.

She tries to imagine how the conversation could go.

Reg: *I found these.*
Richard: *Ah, yes, found those in the woods. Bit weird. Forgot I had them. Ha ha ha.*
Reg: ...

Or
Reg: *What are these?*

Richard: *Reg, it's a terrible mistake, I have these urges. I'll seek help. Don't leave me.*

Reg: …

Or

Reg: *Richard, can you explain this?*

Richard: …

Reg: *Richard?*

Richard (quietly): *I didn't know how to tell you. I love her.*

Reg: …

There's a rich, buttery slant of light that slides through the kitchen window and warms the tiles at about 2pm this time of year. Reg had assumed she'd always be here to see it, every spring until she died or they carted her into a care home. The thought of it makes the back of her throat constrict until she is saturated with unshed tears, unable to move in case they spill out. She needs to rid herself of this feeling. But how?

She stuffs the pants into the mug. Cold tea sloshes out onto the table. Good.

Good but not enough.

Whether he's a pervert, or a rapist, or an adulterer, promises have been broken. Promises made in that grubby little Registry Office. Other, more important promises made in their big white bed: night after night when she woke from shadows bearing down on her. 'It'll be OK, Reggie, I'm here. Nothing can hurt you. Shhh now. Shhh.' Night after night before Matty was born and some nights after too.

She takes her penknife from the drawer, flicks it open. She wants to do damage. She wants to tattoo herself onto Richard's heart. She wants to inflict pain.

How much pain, exactly, does she want to inflict?

The chickens *cluck, cluck, cluck* their way into daylight. It's not the tall, kind man. It's the short, fat woman and something glints in her hand.

Peter Newall

My Last Journey with Baron Baldanders

I had a good number of engagements arranged in cities and towns reaching from Lemberg to Vienna, all put in place by my admirable agent Greta, who must know every theatre director, casino operator and hotel manager in Central Europe. She had busied herself all autumn, setting up an itinerary extending over a thousand kilometres and lasting from January to March, which would, if all went well, not only provide me with a measure of financial security, but also a platform of reputation from which to pursue performances in the biggest venues, London, Milan, even New York.

But before embarking on this programme I decided to take a tour, privately and without publicity, through Galicia, with my usual, I might say habitual, travelling companion, Baron Baldanders.

The Baron was a man of vast education. Indeed, I sometimes wondered whether the sheer weight of his knowledge and experience had made him tired of the world, perhaps even of life. He nevertheless was always ready to see more of it, and as he was an undemanding companion, and I was accustomed to his presence, I invited him to accompany me. Or it may have been assumed between us; I cannot specifically recall inviting him. To tell the truth, I found the Baron's company, after all this time, somewhat enervating, and in theory I would have preferred to be rid of him. But I did not wish to travel alone, and so once again we proceeded together.

The Baron throughout this trip dressed as he would for an evening in the city; a black suit, a stiff shirt with a white tie, and a silk top hat. I was quite used to this, and thought nothing of it; only now it strikes me that nowhere we went, even in the remotest countryside, did anyone, from barefoot stablehands to *maîtres d'hôtel,* show the slightest surprise at his appearance.

So, setting out from Brody, we wandered circuitously through Galicia, the Baron and I. We used as the markers of our journey the larger towns, and some of the more unusual natural phenomena and places of historical interest that lay between them.

It was December, and the weather was bad. The train sufficed for most of our intended destinations, but up in the Carpathian mountains, where the railways do not run, we were obliged to use the roads, or what passed for roads there. Several times our carriage became stuck fast on the way, and we had no help for it but to get out and wait while the coachmen pushed and pulled to free the wheels, the horses' hooves throwing up great clouts of grey mud and snow as they fought to gain purchase. I still remember the sharp, echoing crack of the whips in the freezing air, the horses' snorting, the grunting and swearing of the coachmen as they bent their backs, up to their knees in mud. Most of all I recall the cold that penetrated my heaviest clothing as we stood in the snow, waiting to resume our journey. The worst of it was the pain it brought to my hands, which took a long time to recover their circulation after each of these delays.

The hotels were uniformly poor, and the restaurants likewise; apart from one very good meal of local dishes in a tavern outside Chust, I see no need to recall, still less record, those details of our travels. Indeed, much of it blurs in memory into one long ride, now in carriages, now in trains.

But certain experiences remain with me, beginning with a visit near the start of our explorations. Bypassing for the moment Lemberg, we had reached the town of Drohobycz. The hotel manager recommended a visit to the saltworks there, which he claimed were the oldest in Europe. As gathering experience was part of the justification for our trip, I agreed. Rather to my surprise, the works turned out to be within the town limits; we could have walked there from the hotel, had I known.

The saltworks sprawled over a large area. Around an unpaved, muddy central yard, into which deep, water-filled ruts had been cut by the wheels of carts, stood ten or twelve brick and wooden buildings, each in a greater or lesser state of decay and dilapidation. Snow-covered roofs were holed, walls at a tilt, doors awry. The yard was littered with freshly-cut pine logs, and new yellow sawdust powdered the churned-up slush. Nobody was in sight. Somewhat nonplussed, we entered one of the shanty-like buildings, from which a metal chimney leaked smoke into the thin, pale air.

Inside there was no floor, only packed earth. Under a roof of rusted iron sheets, two or three long, flat, shallow pans stood above wood fires, which burned in brick ovens shaped like upended culverts. The pans contained a thick greyish liquid, which steamed over the flames. Long-handled wooden tools, stirrers or scrapers of some sort, lay around or were propped against the wall. A single heavy mitten, blackened and stiff, sat on a shelf. There was no light except the orange glow of the fires and a few narrow shafts reaching through gaps in the slatted walls. As much smoke coiled around inside as escaped through the chimney, mixing with the steam from the pans. It was a kind of modest Hell.

The liquid, I realised, was salt water. Around the edges of the trays, coarse white grains crusted. I tasted a pinch; it seemed bitter. Unsure what else there was to see, the Baron and I wandered out into a rear yard, where a bedraggled dog bristled and growled, but did not approach us. Under an awning stood uniform rows of fat white sacks, presumably filled with salt.

At that point two men emerged from the darkness of a low doorway. One, the elder, had a heavy moustache and wore a flat cap. The other, a much younger man, had a reddish face with amorphous features and tiny, deep-set eyes. Both wore clothes which were indescribably filthy; it was difficult to be certain exactly what form of garments they were, in fact.

I speak passable Polish and Russian, so usually I can follow the Ruthenian language, but these two spoke in a dialect so thick I understood nothing at all. The Baron, however, asked a couple of questions of the older man, who answered him respectfully, if as it seemed to me reluctantly. Yes, this was the ancient saltworks, it had been in operation for more than a thousand years, the salt water was pumped from sixteen metres below the earth then dried out over fire, the Baron translated for me. It had always been done this way, he added.

The younger man listened, leaning in the doorway at a prodigiously steep angle, his crossed feet against the bottom of one doorpost, his shoulder against the other. Then, in a curious, hesitating sing-song, he addressed the Baron, quite jocularly, almost familiarly. What he said, the Baron did not translate for me, and I did not ask.

The whole scene reminded me forcibly of those paintings by the elder Brueghel of mediaeval European peasant life. Indeed, I thought I could recall seeing exactly this salt-boiling in one of those canvasses, although I could not remember which. The sawn-up logs lying in the muddy, absurdly rutted yard, the raggedy dog, the smoke and snow, the brick ovens, the clumsy old-fashioned tools, were all precisely from

Breughel, but most of all the two men, their faces full of inherited peasant knowledge and brute cunning.

Satisfied we had seen enough, we picked our way back across the yard and took our places in the waiting carriage. Just as we were seated, the dog burst into view, barking furiously, its eyes staring, its fur on end. It stopped just short of us, sitting back on its haunches, but kept up its clamour until we had passed through the gates out onto the paved street.

I was left with the impression that we had physically travelled back in time, back into mediaeval Europe, with its superstitions and short lifespans, its coarseness and cruelty, its dirt, its beauty, its closeness to God.

From that place we roamed through the scattered towns of old Galicia. Bolechów, Nagyszőlős, Perecseny, Lubaczów, Stryj, Halicz, and the rest. In each town, at first by chance and then by unspoken agreement, we searched out the synagogue; this began with our observation of the handsome, green-plastered Choral Synagogue in Drohobycz, and continued as we proceeded south. In every town the synagogue was no longer in use for worship, in most places abandoned and derelict. Nevertheless we contrived to enter most of them and look about, clambering the staircases to the upper floors where we could.

An overwhelming sadness sat heavily in each of these, dusty, silent, buildings, now completely purposeless. It struck me as the sadness of absence, although, as the Baron observed, smiling thinly, there were ghosts everywhere. Even I could sense them, flitting away as we rounded corners and climbed rickety stairs.

In Bolechów we found the synagogue roughly boarded up, but inside, structurally intact. Its internal walls had been painted over a muddy orange, but carelessly, and the overpainting was peeling off in big curling strips. Beneath it we made out portions of frescoes, and in one place a text from the Kashrut, which I copied into my notebook.

These synagogues had become useless all of a sudden, almost unexpectedly, and it seemed the local people hadn't known quite what to do with them. They had no doubt been looted, but then closed up with an odd carelessness, and simply left. Even the boards nailed over the windows, where the glass had been smashed or removed, had been put up haphazardly, allowing thin slivers of grey light to penetrate. In Volove, the porphyry pillars inside – not real porphyry, of course, but well done – still stood. In Borysław, the parquet flooring, although burst and scattered near the door, was within still largely intact; it creaked and clacked underfoot as we walked through the empty rooms.

Near Pustomyty, a Jewish graveyard stood on a steep hillside, the dark stone markers sunk deep into the snow, some upright, some leaning, like candles on a forgotten birthday cake.

As we left the synagogue in Nagyszőlős, which was being used as a sort of barn, half full of disintegrating furniture, three men in army surplus camouflage challenged us, asking for money. They began circling us, shouting in dialect I once again could not understand, although their threats were obvious enough. It was clear why they had chosen us; two well-dressed men investigating a synagogue were likely to be both wealthy and easily cowed. I set out to push past them, but the Baron stopped, felt in his fob pocket, and gave the oldest of them, a barrel of a man with red, inflamed eyes and a clipped grey beard, a coin. The fellow stared down at it for a long moment, then threw it, almost convulsively, to the snowy ground; he stumbled backward, and the three of them turned and hurried away, looking back once before breaking into a shambling run. The Baron did not trouble to retrieve the coin, and we went on our path unhindered.

In Munkács, we ate lunch at the central hotel, the *Andrassy*. In trying to find the bathroom, I came upon a back room behind the kitchen area. On the floor in one corner stood a small rectangular metal pan, shallow, half-full of water, containing two tortoises. The water had not been changed recently, and smelled rank. There was barely room for the two creatures to fit side by side in the pan, and the curved backs of their mottled brown shells protruded above the surface. They lay there, staring straight ahead, moving their legs occasionally.

As I watched, they both, at the same moment, turned their heads inwards to look at each other. I imagined that look to convey something like, 'We are in a damned fix, aren't we, old boy…' I felt extraordinarily sad for them. I sensed some analogy between their situation and that of the departed Jews of all these Galician towns, but I could not bring it to a clear expression.

Our wanderings, interesting though they were, went on rather longer than I had expected. In the end we returned to Lemberg, or possibly Krakow; I was tired by then, and all those mediaeval cities had begun to look the same to me. Wherever it was, we took a suite at the Casino, in the centre of the Old Town.

Our suite was on an upper floor, comprising several rooms, high-ceilinged and without windows. The wallpaper throughout was dark grey, worked with an old-gold pattern. Heavy furniture, mahogany or oak, stood around the walls, wardrobes and chests and carved-backed chairs. The rooms were lit by gas jets; their hissing glow did not reach low enough to illuminate the thick carpets I felt underfoot. I noticed that no single room was formed by right-angles. Each wall met the next at an oblique or acute angle. The ceilings, as a result, were not rectangular, but rhomboidal, and seemed never to form a single plane surface.

Two cats occupied the suite when we entered it, one orange and one black; one sitting high up on the curtain-rod, looking down, the other in the middle of the floor, looking up. They maintained a kind of balance; when one ran up the curtains, the other ran down them. Each time they changed places, they stopped still and hissed at one another. I accepted their presence there without question.

On our first evening, the hotel had arranged a box for us at the local opera theatre, a grand building in a Viennese Baroque style. *Carmen* was playing, an opera I do not much care for, but I must say it was performed with considerable verve. The mezzo-soprano Carmen was no longer in her first flush of youth, but carried herself in a convincingly louche manner, and the whole vocal range of the role, even the lowest registers, fell comfortably within her compass. She deservedly received generous applause.

The thermometer showed minus twelve when we emerged from the theatre, so we did not linger outside, but took a light supper in the restaurant opposite before returning by carriage to the Casino. I was thinking, as we rolled through the snowy streets, that I really would prefer to have some time to myself now, but the Baron was as ever at my elbow. I began to wonder whether it was a weakness to permit him so much to be in my company, when I found his world-weariness to a degree contagious, dampening to my spirits. I had no basis for an open rupture with the Baron, however; if there was a fault in our arrangement, it was hardly his.

Perhaps he sensed my feeling, because we had not long returned when he indicated he wished to rest. His bed was set up in a separate room, a narrow bed with high wooden sides. He lay in it fully dressed, flat on his back, and I placed the requisite wooden cover over him. As I was doing so the two cats approached, conveying a clear desire to climb onto the Baron's bed. I allowed them to, and he made no protest. The crouched together on his chest, and I placed the cover over them all.

Then I sat for a long time in my room, unable to read, as I had intended, but equally unable to sleep, in a state of extreme anxiety about my forthcoming appearances. How could I possibly take the stage? How dare I regard myself as a performer, how dare I ask people to pay to see me, an amateurish bungler, a clumsy hack? I thought of cancelling the tour, of claiming to be ill, anything to avoid appearing. Just at the lowest point of my confidence, a telegram arrived from Greta; she was on her way to see me. I felt, I have to admit, immediately relieved.

Greta is a strong-featured woman who dresses severely and keeps her dark hair cropped short. She goes out of her way to obtain American cigarettes, not always easy to find in this part of the world, which she smokes through an amber holder. Officially she manages my professional career, but the truth is, this management spills over into my life generally, so much do I depend on her judgment.

It must have been well after midnight that Greta was shown to the suite. She greeted me matter-of-factly, and placed the large leather portfolio she carried on a glass-topped side table. Before opening it, though, she went into the Baron's room, I with her, and lifted the lid from his bed.

The Baron was, as before, lying on his back. His pale blue eyes were wide open, bearing a look of pained surprise. There was a huge circular hole in his abdomen, two feet across, neatly cut into his stiff dress shirt, going straight through his body, and dropping down, like a well-shaft, through the bottom of the bed, through the floor, and down into the unguessable depths of the earth. He was, you understand, dead.

Greta, completely unperturbed, told me that the cats we had found resident in our suite are called 'Kilkenny cats,' and that their destiny is to chase each other's tail forever. They are meant to be kept separate, but if allowed to get close together in one spot, they chase each other's tail with such ferocity that they create a whirling circle of colossal speed, going round so fast that it acts like a drill. When I permitted them to sit on the Baron's chest together, they began this chasing, Greta said, and it became so rapid that they bored down through his body like butter. We bent over the Baron – I saw bits of rib and bloody meat on the edges of the big circular hole that had been drilled through him – and looked down into the cylindrical shaft reaching deep into the centre of the earth, which was grey and ashy. The Kilkenny cats were down there, still going round and round at impossible speed.

In a hotel of this class, the staff will clear this away in the morning without comment, Greta said, and we returned to the main room, where we spent some hours over the plans for my forthcoming performances.

While his end might have been thought unfortunate, I was essentially relieved that the Baron had departed. I wished him no ill, but I felt his time with me had properly come to its conclusion. Over the next few days, however, I became intensely aware of his absence. I felt depressed, and, to tell the truth, rather ill. The symptoms were those of withdrawal from addiction: anxiety, headache, sweating, intermittent fever.

The night before I began my schedule of performances, I wrote to my friend Irina Anatolievna in St Petersburg, giving the details of the Baron's demise and my reaction to it. Like most Russian women of her class, she is deeply conversant with arcane matters. She wrote back:

"It does appear that you have seen the last of him, yes. But we must remember him with some respect. He existed, with his own karma; how can we not feel compassion, even for those who would destroy us?

It seems that such as he prefer to hide in plain sight. The tedium you ascribe to your association with him was, I feel, a fan dance of the Baron's; he understood that keeping a low profile aids longevity. But one's nature will show itself, sooner or later, so little by little the Baron's inviolability frayed.

And ask yourself this, why did he come to you in the first place, who ended up the agent of his demise, in such a, may I say, severely prejudicial manner?

I feel that the Baron, for all his vices, protected you, and you are now, with his departure, exposed. Be very careful of anyone unknown who approaches you."

On reading this letter, which I received in my dressing-room in the theatre in Oppeln, I felt sad for the Baron, and sorry for myself. Just as I was folding the small square of pale blue paper away, Greta entered, to tell me that there were twenty minutes until curtain, and that the local Lieutenant-Governor, one Ritter von Kotschek, greatly desired an audience with me after the performance.

The show, I have to say, was a resounding success; I took seven curtain-calls.

Diana Powell

Empathy

She spotted the girl in the yellow dress in the Square that morning. A lemon-sherbet colour, standing out from the crowd. Later, she saw her again, moving through the tables in front of the cafés, where the tourists drank Beirao and Sangria. She noticed other things about her, then – the way her freckled skin and Seville-marmalade hair clashed against her outfit. The slouch of her make-up. The rank of blood.

It was easy to follow her, fixing on the fizzing yellow, ignoring all the greens and reds of the flags, canopies and football-strips pieced against the sky. She wove through the streets toward the harbour, down into the labyrinth of alleyways. The yellow was gone now, but it didn't matter. There was no need for it – or for some ball of thread to show her the way. This close, there never was. Then round a final corner into a deserted dead-end, full of bruised, hulking shadows and strewn bins. She found her sitting amongst the stench of sodden cardboard and pools of food sap, crying. She lifted her up, saying, 'It's okay. I can help you,' and put her arms around her neck.

It was simple to reach her hand beneath the swathe of orange hair, where the fallen nape waited. Her fingers probed, sought, found the clasped steel, and unhooked it, and still the girl didn't flinch – a puppet with cut strings against her shoulder, while Gina unclenched the teeth of the zip, one by one. Down, matching the curve of the chine, down.

And then she was there, at the base, feeling for the bare skin, reaching lower towards the cleft, kneading the flange of bone. Sacred, she'd heard it called.

The place, where it must begin.

She knew what to do.

This was the best way for large mammals, she'd learnt.

There were different names, instructions for smaller creatures – *open* skinning, *case* skinning. But, of course, the human body was a superior specimen, in this, as in everything, and required special attention.

'The *dorsal* method. Not so dissimilar from the *open*, but the creature is laid belly down, back up. The cut follows the spine, or *chine*, where access is easier. You must start at the base.' It was what all the best taxidermists instructed. 'Think of it as an unzipping in reverse.'

Yes, they were talking about bears, and the larger of the apes, and lions and tigers, and yes, her subjects were more often upright than prone, but it had always sufficed for her needs… their needs.

She burrowed her nail inside, twisting it, almost, like the bit of a drill, then slid it upwards, against the way she had come.

It was done.

And yes, another slit down each of the limbs, and the skin fell away, just as the taxidermists said. So easy, so perfect. 'A cleaner method, with less exposure to internal organs.' Yes. And she was glad of that. All she had to do then was pick it up from where it lay on the grimed stony ground, still wearing its yellow shroud, And step inside.

Or… *'This is what it feels like,' she tells him, the latest of men in white coats, who do not wear white coats any more, trying to understand. And 'tell me about your childhood,' he says, as they all say. Where it begins…*

When she was younger, she noticed the birds. The chaffinch, first, flying into the kitchen window. The way the bones of her body jarred out of place from head to foot at the sound, how her nerves shuddered. She found it lying beneath the sill, a single drop of blood at its eye. She curled up beside it, holding her hand to her cheek. Her throat pulsed, matching each beat of the slow rise and fall of its dying.

Her mother found her there, touched her with her toe.

'What are you doing?'

She raised a finger towards the fallen creature.

'It's just a bird. Get up, and help me put these clothes on the line.'

Later, she watched as next-door's cat opened an eye, reached out a paw. The coil of its back, the uncurling of the claw; the pounce. She hadn't seen the sparrow on the lawn, bobbing around for crumbs. There was no noise, not from the bird. It was different, this time. The claw ripping the flesh, the feathers skewed and scattered; the innards scooped. She held her stomach close, wanting to keep her heart, her lungs, her gizzard (did she have a gizzard?) safe inside. To stop the blood.

'It's just nature, tooth and claw and all that shit,' her sister told her. 'You're such a drama-queen!'

And when she looked at her hands, there was nothing.

Birds were different as well. Different, difficult, on account of the feathers, so easily broken and bloodied – and yet needing to be preserved. 'The perfection of the plumage is eminently desired.' Collarbone to cloaca, first. Fine cuts to the side, severing the filigree of muscle fibres, more like a removal of the body than a freeing of the skin. An 'inside-out' version, the creature turned inside out, like a washed sock.

It didn't matter. She knew none of this, then.

As she grew, people around her exploded into reds, oranges, pinks, sending zig-zagging white peaks through her head. Orchestras came from nowhere and burst into syncopated rhythms, forcing her hands to her ears, her eyeballs out.

'How can you stand it?' she asked her sister.

'What?'

That's when she knew it was only her.

For a while, she decided she was a mutant. They were everywhere, staring down from every billboard, bursting out from every screen. T-shirts; backpacks; plastic toys, belonging to her brother, waiting to leap out and puncture bare feet, or trip up anyone 'big'. Super-heroes, super-villains, with super powers. 'Empathy', she would be called – someone who felt too much; someone who took on the pain of others, sucking it from them, suffering in their place. Climbing inside their skin. Yes, that's what she did. Birds had moved on into people. Once, she had seen a man being mugged on the other side of the road. She fell, the breath sucked out of her, soft muscle tissue collapsing with each punch, bones cracking with each kick.

'Help me,' she mouthed. People gathered round her, away from the bruised and bleeding man, then shook their heads and tsk-tsked when they realised there was nothing wrong. Perhaps she wasn't so 'super' after all. Perhaps she should keep 'Empathy' hidden away, out of the gaze of the rest of the world, devise an alter-ego, for everyday use. Something else that all the greatest super-heroes did. Why shouldn't it work for her?

She shut herself inside, as much as any teenage schoolgirl could; quarrelled with her friends, kept her head down when she was out.

'What's wrong with you?' Jess asked. 'You should be out partying!'

Teenage parties, where hormones collided with alcohol and drugs. There could be nothing worse. Besides, she didn't need it, if sex was what she wanted. It was there, in the black box on the other side of the room. It was there, in Jess and her latest, curled up on the sofa, watching. Like she was watching. She heard the silence wrap itself around them, saw their lips flick from side to side, felt them trying to hold themselves in. Felt more, far more, than them, clutching herself tight, hugging herself, as if someone else was there, holding her. Such a good feeling… there, with the couple on the screen; there, with Jess and Arno; there…

She would get up then, and leave the room, and head for her own bed. Not such a bad thing, perhaps – the kicks, without the complications. She knew from school how messy things could be. But knew, too, that real sex would always be too much for her.

Older, late at night, she walked through parks, on the wrong side of town, where she saw the bushes move with cigarette tips, heard breath bated, baited for the men. She waited, too, watching, until…

And she would go home, and crawl into bed, and think, like her teenage self, 'This is good. Sex without complications, without pregnancy, without disease.' Without the arms of a man. Love.

Everything was different after the girl in the yellow dress. The skin had fitted too well; she couldn't escape from it, no matter how hard she tried. Reaching behind her neck, pulling at something that wasn't there, wanting to shed it all again, like some snake sloughing away the parasites that tormented it. The insides should be thrown away, but somehow, they were still there.

The heart, which was ripped in two. The lungs, made to catch the breath, to breathe, to take a breath when things were bad – squeezed to no more than two limp balloons, so that she/she could not breathe, could not take in a single gasp of air. The stomach – that strange organ, supposedly for digestion, yet infested with trembling butterflies, or gut-wrenched.

The womb, where the baby had been, where all the babies had been.

'I can help you,' she had said. 'I know what you're going through. I can share your pain.'

But the girl was too broken, and broke her, too.

Find somewhere peaceful, surrounded by uncomplicated souls,' he tells her. 'Somewhere to repair yourself.' And yes, it makes sense. It is what she needs. And so… here she is.

Now the nuns flap past her, only their moon faces visible. Good. There are no seductive tresses, no visible flesh to worm her way into, no skin, except for their pallid cheeks. And what can happen in this place? A cut to the finger as vegetables are sliced; a twinge in the lower back from digging too long in the flower-beds. Arthritic joints from too much kneeling. These she can deal with – discomfort, no worse.

Only the Christ in the Chapel bothers her, hanging there, splayed on His crucifix. A shard of pain burns both hands, both feet. But she soon learns to lower her eyes, when she enters the hall, as if she is not worthy. And the nuns praise her devotion.

Sister Rose is the first, sidling beside her as she sits at the refectory table. Talking, when she should be silent.

'You know, don't you?'

And she does. She had thought nuns to be virginal, innocent, empty of sin; women who did not want to be part of this world and its cruelty. She was wrong.

'I was young,' Rose says.

'It's good to share,' she adds, as she leaves.

The next day, it's Sister Clara, short, solid, the face of a sprouting potato. The nun who works in the garden.

'It wasn't my fault. It was with his consent. The judge understood that, and was lenient. Perhaps he had the same tastes… But I knew I must shut myself out of harm's way – their harm, my harm. Which is why I came here.'

'I'm so glad you understand.'

And she does. She understands them all.

Sister Hope.

Sister Faith.

Sister Charity.

All.

Soon, the priest who comes once a week to hear their confessions, sits lonely in his box. They have no need of him now.

They have her.

She sits in a cell at the top of the tower. She has told the Mother Superior she wishes to increase her devotion, though vows were never her intention when she arrived. The walls are bare – she has removed the crucifix and hidden it under the bed. Her meals are left outside the door – a door of hewn oak, dense. Nothing can get in. They can't get in, without her consent.

It is quiet here, and she can breathe.

And there is the window.

She can stand at the window, and look at the sky and the sea. There is nothing else there.

Except the birds.

She had forgotten about the birds.

She has forgotten about the chaffinch, that first awakening. Or the sparrow, torn apart by a single claw. It is easy enough when her head is busy trying to rid itself of the years of other people's pain. She remembers them now, but it doesn't matter – there are no cats here, no glass in her window. And the birds are quite different from the common garden variety, clamouring too close to humans and their pets, in the hope of an easy meal. So it is pleasant to watch these birds catching the breeze, skimming the water, spiralling upward, downward. The confidences of the Sisters lighten, fade.

And soon she is flying with them, gliding, crying into the heavens. She sees all species of seabird, travelling between the cliffs. Fulmars, petrels; gannets trailing the dolphins; cormorants following the fish. She especially likes the terns, the shimmy of their forked tails, their buoyant grace, their feathers silver in the morning sun; how they hover before their dive. Yes, today she is happy to be inside the lone tern as it dances above the white horses, then picks up speed, to catch up with the rest of the flock. Flick, dart, rush. She might even forget the girl in the yellow dress today.

She/it hasn't noticed the falcon, coming from the cliffs. It is too fast, perhaps, for sight. But there is her sense, the tern's sense. The bird flies faster, she is with it, straining forward, further, on, out, yearning to put space between it and its predator; leaning out from the window, towards the water, the jagged rocks that form the shore. She climbs out onto the window ledge, to be closer still.

The falcon rises high above. Good, it is gone. She can breathe again. The tern can slow for now.

'The peregrine is the fastest of birds in its downward swoop. Once it has fixed its prey in its sight, there is nothing to be done.' She has learnt a lot about birds in her studies of skinning them.

Down it comes, claws clenched, like Sister Clara's hands.

The tern falls, as the talons hook deep inside its flesh.

And if the tern falls, so must she.

In empathy.

Anju Sharma

Things we see, things we don't

Come, look, what happened.

I had just woken up and was still orienting myself, when I heard my husband call me. I went outside rubbing my eyes. He was staring at something. He pointed at it with his chin.

What is it? I said, squinting at the thing he showed.

*

Our neighbor's dog had a litter some time back. Now the puppies made their way in, through the iron grille of our gate. In the beginning we shooed them away. They shat everywhere and chewed on our badminton shuttles. But our daughter loved to play with them. She fed them pao with her hands. The four of them clambered on her, soon as they saw her. She rubbed their bellies and they rolled on their backs.

I wasn't sure if the neighbors liked the idea of the pups playing in our yard. I checked with them. They didn't have a problem. As long as you are okay with it, they said. Of course, we are! I nodded quickly. My daughter is in love with them.

Our daughter was an only child. We had tried for another, but all the hope there was had petered out by now. I was forty-two. It felt too late and it *was* in many ways too late. Still, it did something to me, to watch our daughter go from one room to the other aimlessly, to hear her talk to herself, to see hope on her face at the slightest sound of any children in the vicinity.

I felt doubly guilty. She had been asking for a pet for long. I didn't grow up with dogs or cats, and my mother's resistance now ran in my blood. Besides, who was going to do the dog's work? The answer was *me*! And one thing I knew by now – what could be put off, should be put off. Because if it wasn't, it was sure to land on my shoulders. My shoulders seemed like a safe place to everyone. I could stumble with weight, but I'd never let anything fall – this is what I think everyone felt.

The pups' mother was now a frequent visitor too. We called her Machu. Machu was a timid looking dog who surprised us with her impatience with the pups sometimes. She snarled and pawed at them when they came at her constantly. But she stood still like a pole when they nursed at her. So still, it seemed the breeze stopped with her. We too would stop talking then and move away from the scene.

Once my husband dragged around a dried palm frond to pile in the backyard, when Machu nursed the puppies. I was upset with him. This could wait! I said. He looked at me, puzzled. I pointed at the mother and her hungry babies. He looked back at me with his mouth open.

What am I doing to them?

They will be distracted. Machu may get frightened, I said.

They're dogs for godsake, he said. They don't think like you and me.

No. We are dogs. I had to control my voice so not to shout. Don't you see that? I was so angry my breath went haywire. I had to come inside the house and sit.

*

Back to the morning when our daughter still slept and my husband called me outside. *Come, look, what happened.*

I stared at what he showed me. My bra lay in the middle of our small front yard. It was a white bra gone greyish, dingy. I had a mind to throw it for many months, but I hadn't. The bra was lightly padded, like all my bras were, and it had a finger size hole near to the hooks, where fabric had given way with too much use. Of course, you couldn't see any holes or runs, standing afar. But the first thought I had, soon as I could focus – how ugly it looked! It lay there, splayed. The cups inverted – like filthy bowls of a poor, hungry person.

It's the puppies done it, my husband said. I looked at the clothes stand in the veranda. All the other clothes were in place. The underwear and lingerie went on the lower rack and with its hanging straps, the bra made for an easy target.

Just then a puppy squeezed in through the gate and ran to the bra. At that point, I made a dash for it too, stomping my feet as I walked. The pup ran and hid under the car. I picked up the bra and without stopping to look anywhere or at the bra itself or at my husband as I walked past him, I came back into the house and went straight for the trash bin. As I walked, I knotted it over and over again until it became a sort of pokey ball. I pushed it deep into a corner of the bin, until it couldn't be seen from the top.

*

This happened many years ago. Eighteen about. This was a time I lived with – now it's hard to use the words, but yes, my family. In fact, we were on our way to become more of a family and didn't know it then. When my daughter played with those pups – within one year from that time, she became a sister. We became parents again.

My pregnancy was an exciting time for her. She was filled with questions about my rounded belly and the baby that rested inside it. Through references in the visual dictionary we had at home, she kept a track of the various stages of a baby's growth in the womb. She learnt too much really, looking into that dictionary day and night those days. With my swollen feet and persisting backache, I could hardly keep a track of what she was up to.

I remember the letter she wrote to God and showed me. Dear God, please give me a sister. Please please please! If it is a boy, I will put him in a cage. Don't be upset with me then.

It was a boy. There was a small tantrum in the beginning, as expected, but soon she was playing with the baby. Helping swaddle him. Taking pictures. Carrying him in the crook of her little arms, from one room to the other. My mother, who came to live with us for a few months, walked close on her heels, anxious.

*

I was cleaning my closet today. Folding and arranging clothes in separate piles. Balling up the socks. Making neat little folds of bras and panties. Actually, not so little anymore as far as panties went – my panties were XL size now and in solid colors mostly. Bras for sure had become smaller without padding. I couldn't suffer the heat of foam on my breasts anymore, or wires, or the look of lace against my skin. I couldn't suffer bras at all.

It was while I was sorting this stuff, that the image of a dull, sad looking white bra on the ground, in the open, came to me. My husband's voice came to me – *Come, look, what happened.*

My husband lived with someone else now. About the time our daughter was finishing school and our son was eight or so, he started making frequent trips to the town his parents lived in. They were old, a slew of sufferings – knee transplant, angioplasty, hipbone fracture, fear of the unforeseen. At one point, he lived with them more than he lived with us. A decision was made then to put our younger one in boarding – our daughter was ready to leave home for college anyway. We went doing a recce of schools. I had pangs on those long drives. He was still small. It felt as though I was trying to change the course of water. It took everything I had, to go with the idea of sending our son away.

Indeed, there was freedom after that. It felt ill begotten, but there it was, shining like goldfish in a bowl. I began to write seriously. My husband's visits home increasingly lessened, and then arrived the long mail from him, explaining the peace and the sense of calm he had found in a new relationship. In fact, it was a very old relationship. He had known this person from childhood. They lived in the same gated community as kids, their families were friends, and both sets of parents had later built homes on plots next to each other's. Her marriage was long over. No children in the picture. She had come back to live with her parents just like him.

I had met her too – in the days we visited my husband's parents' house as family. She was a lively person, full of anecdotes. She had a way of laughing that everyone laughed just looking at her, no matter the joke.

In the mail my husband wrote, he assured me there hadn't been anything between them, all the past years. Not when he and I were together, not before that. But now he couldn't say the same. Of course, I wrote back to him. I know you better than that. I know it's the one thing you haven't done – lying to me. I appreciate the sharing of development, I wrote. About time we lived exactly as we pleased. You have my blessings. I added a smiling and a folded hand emoji.

Only once, just once, during the time all of this was happening, I had shut the door to my bedroom –

although I lived alone and there wasn't a need to do that – and I howled. I beat the pillows. I made sounds that frightened my own ears. I had to bite my arm to be quiet. I shook with anger, with fear, with such shimmery loneliness that I thought – I didn't think, I felt – I was disappearing.

*

I moved to the hills, not far from my son's boarding school. The house was anyway a rental. There were a few bank accounts in my name. The money in them is all yours, my husband said. He said not to hesitate to ask for more, if there's need. Sure, of course, I said.

Our children went out of the country – our daughter left for the US for her Masters, and our son joined an IB program in Singapore. Their father funded them, assisted them through the admission process. He took complete charge, made it a mission to have it work out for them.

I said to him, in the days he and my daughter were thick into applications to American Universities, if helping too much was really a help. She hadn't qualified for the scholarship. I wondered if any of this – which college, where – mattered in the long run. I think things like these just fall away, I said to him. That everyone was exposed equally in the end, and what remained, what you could hope to hold on to, was something that you always had, something so pure and so silent that you were astonished to know it sprung from you.

No one was interested in the long run or this kind of talk. My husband said – Can you even hear yourself? We are talking about our children's future here! According to him, the very basis of my thinking was wrong. Of course it mattered! he said. In any run - long or short. Where you went, what you did, who you met. These are things of the world and as long as you are living in the world, they matter. Besides, he said, I'm doing the running around, I'm spending the money. Why don't you just relax! Let the children live their best lives, he said. Their lives don't have to be like yours.

*

I went to the US for the first time when my daughter had a baby. She married her colleague from the law firm she worked for. He was Korean-American. A quiet man who smiled easily. They travelled to India for a temple wedding and later organized a small celebration back in Atlanta where they lived. My husband attended it. My daughter said, if I wanted to give it a miss it was alright, but later when she really needed me to be there, to *please, please* make myself available.

Are you expecting? I asked her, my voice small. She laughed. Will you be too mad if I said I was? Come on, that stage is long gone, tell me, I said. Yes! my daughter replied, her voice had a tinkle of bells in it – a loud, merry, ringing, joyful voice that struck fear in me. A sort of cold dismay flooded my chest on hearing her.

It's only the second month. You know, there was the option to… but Sam and I held on to it. He loves children. And besides, isn't it a good idea to just have them and be done with it, she said brightly.

I had decided there and then, listening to her, that come what may, no matter what, I will fly to be with my daughter when she becomes a mother. I hated to travel but my resolve was clear. Moment those words had come out of her mouth – *have them and be done with it* – I knew I'd have to be there. Forget about my routine, my schedule, my deadlines, when it happens. I had to be there to see her through the early days. I had to be there to absorb some of her befuddlement, to be the padding for the fall.

She did the tickets, put me in touch with an agent for the paperwork. This was my first trip to my children's adopted country – my son was now a sophomore at the same university my daughter attended – and I was struck by the scale. Everything was so wide, spread out, so large and tall – it seemed to send out a message about the obstinacy of human spirit. Even the skies didn't seem like the same skies back home, sun not the same sun.

But inside the house, it was the same old story. I stayed with my daughter for six months. Enough time for her to get used to the new reality, establish a routine, put a system in place. I hadn't handled a baby since my own children were small and felt a little nervous, but tried not to show it. My daughter must have sensed this somehow and in spite of the disarray she was in, in spite of the way she swung between extreme agitation and long vacuous stares, she still took the lead at times and I drew confidence from her.

I gave the baby oil massages. We bathed her together. I burped the baby after her feeds. By the time baby was three months old, she was grabbing our fingers and smiling at us. Her left cheek dimpled when she smiled. I played peekaboo with her and loved to hear her chuckle. I could go on and on. The baby was pure joy. But at some point, I began to miss the absence of people around me. My quiet life stood at the window, waiting. I longed to be back home.

My daughter's partner was very supportive, and this was a solace. I had learnt to call him her Partner, as she liked me to. Isn't it in effect, the same thing as husband? I asked her. Partner was neither here nor there, I thought. No, it's not, she said. The words we use, work on us and cast us into their shape and sound and feeling. Some words simply carry a burden on their back. Husband is one of those words, she said.

She was sure, she said, it didn't start off as one, although she will have to go deep into etymology for that – but *Husband* wasn't innocent any longer. The word connoted entitlement. Whereas *Partner* was about teamwork, about equal stakes. Not to say it guaranteed anything, of course not, it's naïve to think that, she said. But if you rested the relationship on good semantics to begin with, you at least did something!

You have to be vigilant from the start, mother, my daughter looked at me and said, or you can't complain later. She spoke while expertly changing nappies. I looked at her and nodded continuously. Hearing my daughter speak this way, always had something rise in me. Love of course, pride. But fear too.

I wished desperately to put a band around her. I wished her words landed soft and sweet in some obscure, lost place. That no one heard them. That they were not taken as challenge to life's authority. Surely, there were so many who were spared. Surely.

But you had to wish for all of this like it wasn't a wish. This prayer I sent out for my children, had to blow like a breeze through me. Little pill that dissolved in water and disappeared. If it gained any weight, it could invite attention. You couldn't do that. You couldn't invite attention. You couldn't be so foolish.

*

I have to confess – sometimes there was an urge to stop my children in their track with the simplest, barest words. Words that were clean, unadorned, that did the job of having them know. Of course, I never did that.

You couldn't have anyone *know* anything. And let's say if you could, if there was someone who could have others know something, I definitely wasn't that person. I was no good at speaking. Words coiled in a place far deeper than my tongue. I could only write.

If I could speak, words wouldn't stop coming on the day I heard my husband call me – *Come, look, what happened*. On the day I saw him watch my bra lay ridiculous in the front yard.

That morning when he came back into the house, I had pushed it down the trash bin already. On seeing him, my mouth opened to say something, but not one word came out. Then I didn't want to look at him – at least not that day. If I looked at him, I wanted to stare at him. I wanted to know about us, what lived in the space between us.

It was morning. Time for activity. Time for newspaper boy, time for milkman. Bread was delivered in the morning. It was time when some neighbor or the other passed on their morning stroll and waved at us if we were outside.

But it wasn't about that. People came or didn't, they saw or not, it mattered, but not really. The bra looked like a body part losing life, turning ashen. It looked pathetic. I had walked in a daze to the bin, unable to shake off the profile of my husband looking at it. He was there before me. He was six steps from it. He was the person who had unhooked my many bras.

I wanted to understand something. At least be able to articulate somehow the dumb amazement I felt. But I wasn't able to do a thing. I remember that I put myself to work. Cleared the dish rack. Wiped the kitchen slab and stove. Rinsed the mugs. Picked out tomatoes and cucumbers to chop. Brushed the crumbs off the dining table cover and placemats. The brush wasn't enough. I picked every little shard of the crumbs stuck to the cloth, between my thumb and my finger. And I remember, as I did that, I muttered thank you thank you thank you under my breath, over and over, over and over. I couldn't stop it.

Lui Sit

Forecast for Rain

The day the dead grandmothers blew into our street, it was my birthday. I was getting ready for my party when the phone buzzed. It was Muriel on the street WhatsApp. Muriel's always on the street WhatsApp when something happens.

OMG. Dead grandmothers.

What?

R U ok?

There's one stuck in Luke's tree. Go look.

Despite my better sense, I went outside. It was so windy I had to hold my dress down with both hands which was annoying. I don't normally wear a dress with a full circle skirt but it was my birthday.

The street was chock full of dead grandmothers. Some were perched on the tiled rooftops, alongside the pigeons who didn't seem too bothered. Others were stuck in the fence railings, bordering the neighbours' front gardens, their limbs fluttering in the wind. They were paper thin, semi-translucent, like giant leaves. Except they were animated, chatting to one another. A flock of them were floating across the road, blocking traffic.

The cars didn't know what to do. Drive through or back up and go around. There was lots of honking from the motorists too far back to see what was going on. They should have driven through. After all, they couldn't kill them again.

'Excuse me,' I said to one wearing a green knit vest. 'What's going on?'

She had a tough, lined face. I wasn't surprised she was dead.

'You tell me,' she barked, a smoker's voice if I ever heard one.

'Will you be gone by midday?'

My party was due to start then but she spiralled off in a sudden gust before she could answer.

'It's a sign, it's a sign.' Muriel's unmistakeable whine reached my ears as I neared her house. She was on her knees in her front garden, amongst the many rose plants she adored and was forever pruning.

Her robe wasn't belted and I could see the edge of a satin lace slip beneath. I didn't know what was more shocking. A throng of the dead or that Muriel wore satin to bed.

'A sign of what?' but Muriel just kept rocking back and forth on her heels in an impressive squat.

'Is that your grandmother?'

I pointed to Luke's olive tree across the road where a grandmother was stuck. Her upper body flapped along with the wind, her legs suckered between branches. The family resemblance was clear.

'She used to whip me,' Muriel whispered.

Standing over her, I could see her white roots showing, reminding me that the wind was ruining my blow dry. Holding back my hair, I saw all the neighbours outside, each one talking to, I presume, their dead grandmother.

'Oh no, oh no.' Muriel was moaning and it was getting on my nerves. I looked at my watch and noticed two displeasing facts. It was already 9:38am so I was running late to pick up my birthday cake and I had only moved 753 steps so far. The back of my head was starting to pulse. No. This would not do.

I pulled Muriel out of her squat, onto her feet. Dead or alive, no grandmothers were going to ruin my birthday party. Not again. I tilted my head up to the sky. It looked pale and clear.

'It's forecast for rain,' I lied. 'Go inside Muriel.'

The drive to the bakery took twice as long as usual, the congestion terrible with all those dead grandmothers drifting through the streets. Council workers with industrial strength leaf blowers shifted them along but they'd just blow over to the next street and jam up traffic there. It took forever until one bright soul had the idea to corral them all into the recreation centre and lock them in.

Billy had the cake waiting, iced to perfection. **Happy Birthday Dina** in bright green icing. I beamed, it was exactly how I liked. It resembled all the birthday cakes I'd had since sixteen, each one made by Billy. His technique was flawless. It should be. He'd had enough practice.

'Hey Dina. Everyone's late to pick up orders today. What am I going to do with their dried-out cake?'

I shook my head.

'You know you can count on me Billy.'

'I could set my watch by you. You having your party still?' His hand fluttered in the air as he spoke, too similar to the fluttering going on outside.

I gave him a look which made him fumble at the till as I paid. The shop front was dark despite it being daytime, the windows were inches thick with grandmothers blown up against them.

'Sorry,' he mumbled. 'I should know nothing stops your party.'

Another customer held the door open for me as I passed, my hands full of cakebox. I saw the grandmother stuck on her back as I passed but I didn't say anything. She'd find out herself soon enough.

My party always starts at noon. The blue striped marquee looked so pretty against the backdrop of the wisteria blossoming along the back fence.

Everything was ready, the hor d'oeuvres, the alcohol. The Sonos at the exact volume background music should be played. The scene was so perfect, it seemed a shame to ruin it with guests.

By 12:22, not one guest had arrived. I am a stickler for punctuality, everyone knows. For unforeseen events, one must adapt and accommodate accordingly, that is basic military strategy is it not? But no, they were all late, bleating excuses. Blaming the wind, the traffic, the congestion, anything but themselves. The only things that arrived on time were grandmothers drifting across the garden, blown through by the easterly breeze.

'Don't mind us,' they shouted, wedged amongst the hedges and fencing. 'We'll be on our way again once the wind picks up.'

I didn't respond. It's so rude to gate-crash a party.

It pains me to admit that the party was a bust. For starters, the guests were all distracted, bumping into each other, the chairs, the tables, all because they were looking up instead of out. The small talk was all about why the grandmothers had arrived, revealing conspiracy theorists amongst my social circle. It got so heated, I had to interrupt Eleanor, her face aflame with alcohol, from browbeating Simon.

'It bloody well is,' she shouted at the poor man as I led her away and sat her down with a glass of water.

'It is, don't you think?' she whimpered, her bleary eyes looking into mine. 'A miracle.'

'I don't agree with miracles Eleanor. Now sit there until you can stand again.'

I left her to it only to see Rashaan walk straight into the compost heap at the far end of the garden. I was halfway across to pull him out before I remembered.

'It's just a compost heap now,' I told myself. I doubt Rashaan even noticed being three vodkas in. He'd always been a lush, even at college.

'Best you get out of there,' I shouted, loud enough to pierce his white spirit haze. 'There's maggots and all sorts.'

The intrusion from the grandmothers forced me to end the party early. The guests were too drunk to notice them after a few hours but my nerves were stretched thin. I even forwent the cake cutting which is my favourite part.

By late afternoon, I'd cleared up the mess and sat in the garden to have some prosecco. The scent of cloves mixed with cinnamon entered my nostrils just as I finished the second bottle.

'No.'

I spoke as one speaks to a toddler, but the scent grew stronger, insistent, as if she were standing next to me, her hand resting on my shoulder as it often did towards the end when she couldn't stand unsupported.

'No.'

I gritted my teeth but it did no good.

'Why so sad love, it was a good shindig wasn't it? Nice way to see in your 40s?'

'What are you doing here?'

'I should be asking you that question.'

'It's my birthday.'

'You think I don't know that.'

'Are you determined to ruin every birthday. Wasn't one enough?'

'You know I didn't mean to Dina.'

The way she said my name made me turn to find her but there was no-one there.

'Why can't I see you?'

The alcohol had untethered me, the words slipping out before I could stop them. Her husky laugh filled the garden. I hadn't heard it for years.

'You can. I'm everywhere.'

'I can't.'

'Isn't it time to let it go Dina?'

My name again. Hearing her say it made me open a third bottle. Despite my better sense, I looked over at the compost heap where I had last seen her alive. It had not been a compost heap then but a fire had burned there that evening. Woodsmoke and ash drifting upwards alongside the fumes from the spliff being passed between my friends and I. I had told her to make herself scarce but she didn't listen. It was embarrassing having her at my party. She stunk of booze. I thought grandmothers were supposed to be sweet and doddery. Not mine.

'Do you want to ask me anything?'

'No. I just want to drink in peace.'

'It's ok to miss me love.'

'This is pointless.'

'Don't you want to know what would've happened if you'd been....'

'STOP. Does dying make you psychic?'

'Perhaps,' but I had stopped listening, squinting across the perimeter fence, calculating how much wire netting I would need to make my garden grandmother proof. I drank faster to stop her talking. To stop her face appearing, flushed open with liquor, laughing as she tripped too close, falling onto the flames. I could not swallow fast enough to block the screaming, the squelch of running feet across the sodden lawn. The smell of burning embers and ash, so much ash, floating up, blowing across the back fence.

The chill was thick in the air was when I stumbled to bed, making sure all the doors and windows were locked behind me.

The grandmothers hogged the news, radio, and social media much like they were hogging the outside. After a few days, I stopped following the latest announcements, it was too distracting and it was bad enough with Muriel going kamikaze on WhatsApp, giving updates every time one blew past her window.

Weeks in, the shape of everyday silhouettes changed. Trees, traffic lights, fencing, roof aerials, all bulged with errant grandmothers stuck on them, requiring manual removal or a gust of strong wind to whisk them away elsewhere.

I got used to them, put off at times by the whiff of cinnamon and clove, but I learned to ignore it. After the week of storms came and cleared out a whole load of them to the coast, I could see the shape of the trees lining the streets for the first time in weeks.

At first, the silence felt uncomfortable, other worldly even. But then everything settled down and the news moved onto the latest murder scandal, and even Muriel didn't pay it much mind for she had a new boyfriend. I hope he's fond of satin.

The wire netting arrived this week. It had been delayed because of the weather. I'm going to put it up this weekend with Rashaan's help although the man has no sense of spatial awareness. It's just what I need to make my next birthday party perfect, without any distractions.

Zakia Uddin

Hotline

Altair has a hotline to God, Daisha's mother said before sending her to the isolated house in Sangupur.

Did he say that? Daisha asked. She had seen the phrase only a week earlier in England, on a plastic banner outside of a church. Do you want a hotline to God? Call 0800 1999 1999. She remembered because it was the same digits as the year, making it sound like a time-limited offer.

You can call him uncle, her mother said. She lay in bed, where she'd been since arriving in Sylhet.

He's very religious but still modern. A powerful man: he's going to build a bridge from Sangupur one day, she carried on. He has a family house near your great-aunt. I'll collect you as soon as I'm better.

Altair picked Daisha up from the townhouse in Sylhet. He seemed only in his twenties, too young to be so important. Alone, he and Daisha took a taxi to where men rowed travellers to nearby villages. On the boat to Sangupur, Altair asked Daisha questions in English: would she miss her mother who had stayed behind in the townhouse? Did she like Bangladesh so far? Did she miss home? He answered for her when she hesitated. Her animation in English made her feel clumsy and self-conscious. Her Sylheti was faltering and child-like, but it was almost easy to be with him. He didn't expect her to talk and he never seemed confused when she did.

The bankside hawkers thinned out and the trees thickened as they slid from the city. Altair's eyes were the colour of sucked green pastilles in the steady afternoon light. From the river, he pointed out an old temple and then his own house half an hour later. A red roof flashed distantly between treetops before disappearing. He started speaking rapidly to the boatman and she could no longer follow what he was saying.

When they arrived at the small dock, Altair gestured for her bag. She held onto it; the bag was light, clothes given by her aunts, her baggy jeans and hoodies from London unsuited to the weather. He glanced back now and then but otherwise walked ahead up the incline and into the forest. The dank path was loud with birds. After twenty minutes of padding, a mottled building loomed out of a widening gap. This is your old family home, Altair said, when they reached the edge of the giant clearing.

The veranda of the building was the length of two semi-detached houses in England. Before he could knock, a round woman with yellowing hair and keys dangling from her waist opened the large central door and squinted out of the dusty dark. Don't you recognise me, moyna, *princess*? she asked, propping her walking stick against the doorframe. She thumped Daisha's back and rested her hands on the protruding outline of Daisha's bra.

Of course, Daisha lied. This must be her great-aunt. The ancestral home had long been vacated by her dead father's family. Now only Farah lived there.

Farah took hold of Daisha's bag. She led her through a mote-filled reception stuffed with glass cabinets and out into a quad full of fleeing chickens. They arrived at a large room at the top of the square. You'll share with me, she said, pointing her stick inside. The room accommodated a grand bed and a dining table that could seat six people. There was another small room inside it through which she glimpsed a pink toilet and sink. *En suite*, Farah said, nodding.

Can I sleep on my own? Daisha asked. Don't you like me, moyna? This is aaram, Farah said. She stepped inside and gestured for Daisha to follow. *Com-for-table*, she said, spreading her arms. When she left, Daisha closed the door. She was alone for the first time since leaving Sylhet that day. Her great-aunt pushed the door open again with the stick and shook her head before moving further up the quad.

Daisha listened to Altair and Farah through the barred window. We're so alone here. We need you nearby. You're so good with the young people – although fourteen is not young, Farah said. Her voice was angled at the bedroom for Daisha's benefit. Daisha realised that her great-aunt expected her mind to be kept ajar like the door. When Altair left without saying goodbye, Daisha felt both relief and disappointment that his interest in her had been exaggerated.

*

Farah asked why Daisha wanted to sleep by herself after so many years away. Don't you love your great-aunt, moyna? After Daisha put on her cotton pyjamas, Farah inspected her from behind. It's too much, she said, pointing to Daisha's lower half, miming an hourglass. She pulled out a vast orange maxi dress from the almirah where Daisha had thrown in her gifted clothing.

In bed, Farah kept turning in her sleep, her body shuddering and whistling. The locked room was woozily black from under the mosquito net. The mesh tickled Daisha's sweaty feet; Farah's arm flopped onto her waist. Daisha wriggled until she was nose-first against the clammy nubbed wall and there was a clear inch or two finally between them. Her dreams were frantic and peopled: damp car parks; graffitied shopping centres; starch-collared restaurant workers and their wives gathered in cluttered rooms before their shifts, saying *girls run free when there is no man at home.*

*

After a few days her great-aunt tasked her with shelling beans and feeding the hens. But Farah found overseeing chores so stressful that she insisted on doing most of them herself, only retiring for her lengthy midday nap. Daisha explored the house when her great aunt was sleeping. She rifled through the cabinets full of gifts from visiting relatives. She pocketed dried out cigarettes, a small portable radio, and a blush-pink romance in English. She read it in the evenings before bed. The creased cover had a picture of a busty white woman and an unshaven white man with his tie undone. Daisha peeled her split ends in a drowsy trance after re-reading the dog-eared pages.

*

One morning Farah was nowhere to be found when Daisha woke up. Propping the front door open, she ventured towards the blue waterlogged fields that lay in the opposite direction to the river. Farah appeared in the distance. She raised her stick to indicate that Daisha go back inside. Daisha later learnt that her great-aunt sometimes rushed to her husband's grave if she had news to share, such as having her first guest in months. When Farah returned, she told Daisha never to go outside on her own. Why not? Daisha asked. Anything could happen out there, Farah said. When Daisha asked what the *anything* was, the older woman looked away.

*

Daisha was standing in the quad, her hand buried in a bowl of wet brown peelings and rotting jackfruit when Altair appeared. Your great-aunt has got you labouring, he said. It was the first time he had spoken to her since the boat trip two weeks earlier, even though he had visited since to pass on messages from the city. He was wearing his smart black shoes and white shirt, but he didn't seem to be in a rush.

Her arm fell limply to her side each time as if she was a performer without directions. Altair took the metal bowl from her and went to a shady corner where a few hens and the short-legged cockerel had gathered. She wiped her palms on the side of her salwar kameez, discreetly sniffed them.

Altair's high cheekbones gleamed in the heat. He stuck out his full lower lip to blow off some strands stuck to his forehead. Translucent in the light, his white shirt showed the straight line of his back. When he turned suddenly, it took her a few seconds to realise that she was staring.

Some for the shy chickens, he said, returning. I'm going into town. Do you have a message for your mother or aunts? he asked.

It must get lonely here, he said, when she didn't reply. You always look worried. Your great-aunt is the sleeping lady, you're the busy mind lady. No one for you to chatter with. We can have carefree talks, no? We know each other, he said.

I suppose so, she said. They didn't know each other, but she didn't mind the idea.

Everyone knows you because they know where you're from, one of her aunts had said. The aunt didn't mean everyone knew Daisha or England, which almost everyone here called London. She had meant that Daisha was from Sangupur - even though she had never been there before - because her father had been and people from Sangupur had to be respectable. But when Altair said that he knew her it didn't sound like a warning.

Are you worried about your mother? he asked.

No, she's fine. She's always fine.

You don't think she is ill?

She's not *ill*, as in *sick*.

She is *de-pressed*, he said. It is very hard looking after a young girl on her own.

How do you know?

I know - your mother told me. I know what it is like being your age. Other girls come here to visit, they're also unhappy.

She imagined him talking to other girls. If only they were all here!

Think of this as a calming holiday, not a punishment, Altair said.

The word *punishment* soured the air. His head was lowered as if he was listening to a noise that only he could hear. What would you be doing in England? Anything more exciting than this? he asked. He handed her the empty bowl.

*

One afternoon, Daisha used a spare key that she had found in one of the cabinets to sneak out of the house. She could hear her great-aunt snoring as she left. She walked out onto the field and came across an old split bucket. Sitting on it, she began to smoke. The dried-out tobacco scorched her throat. She turned on the radio. The hook from a pop song she didn't like resounded in the air. She had made fun of it for sounding so stupid and sentimental, but now the nonsensical, insistent lyrics made her feel homesick.

Not long before the summer holiday began, she and her friends had worked their way through old videos, living room curtains drawn: The Devils, The Exorcist, Rosemary's Baby. When they weren't watching films, they hung out in the park smoking weed. An old man who ran The Taj Mahal restaurant nearby saw her with a boy, a friend - not even the one she had got a hold of a few weeks earlier - and told her mother. He confirmed what all the elders in the town suspected: that she was out of control and her mother needed help. After many phone calls, her mother announced that the pair of them were going abroad for the summer to stay with her sisters.

*

The following week, Altair arrived unexpectedly before dinner. He stood in the doorway of the bedroom, a brightly coloured cardboard box in one hand.

I picked up some snacks from the city, he said. Just a small thing.

Farah gestured towards one of the chairs.

How will I feel if I don't feed you? People will gossip! she said.

He peered down at the table and then entered effortfully to show that he was humouring them.

Daisha waited for him to greet her, but he spoke only to her great-aunt.

I've persuaded the planners to draw up blueprints for the bridge, he said after they finished eating. Big changes like this start slowly and then they accelerate, he said.

Farah loudly sucked the marrow out of a thigh bone.

Maybe then *someone* will come to visit us out here,

she said.

Daisha's mother will be visiting in a few weeks, he said. She is a little better, getting out of bed now and then, he said.

Will we go back to Sylhet together? Daisha asked.

Give her some time. Let her be taken care of, he said.

He spoke about her mother's illness as if it was real. But feeling sorry for her mother was like admitting that everyone was right: that it was Daisha's fault for making her sleep all day.

No one has time for an old woman, Farah said. She went to the kitchen, closing the door behind her so that she would hear if anyone left without her permission.

I know you're thinking about when you will escape this place, Altair said when he and Daisha were alone.

The hot bright light of his sudden gaze made her want to brush something off her face.

He looked out towards the yard. Soft black and no footsteps.

God understands all languages, he said, lowering his voice. You can talk to him when you're alone. I'm always talking to him.

What do you talk about? Daisha asked. She thought only very young and very old people believed in God, because that was when you wanted someone to tell you what to do. How was he so sure that God was listening to him?

They say that you've got a special connection, a special gift, Daisha said, when he didn't reply. But he didn't laugh or look flattered as she expected.

Who says that? he asked.

My mother. My aunts.

I talk to God about everything. He has gifted me, it is true. I even talk to him for other people. I can tell him when you're worried or upset, he said.

Why can't I just talk to him directly? In a prayer or something? Daisha asked.

Altair leaned forward, so she could smell aniseed on his breath. The room dipped in and out of shadow as a moth circled the exposed bulb.

First you listen, he said, then you ask.

*

The next evening, Daisha took measured steps towards the pond at the back of the house. The only non-human noises she heard came from the animals. She was unnerved by the invisible birds shaking the canopies and the darkness behind the screen of trees. Behind the pond was a rubbish dump where she had been told to throw her used sanitary towels when she needed to. The needling smell mixed with that of rotting fruit. She took off her sandals and salwar kameez and waded into the water. When she peeled the wet layers of her underclothes, they slapped on again like bandages.

She ran a hand up her calf. Altair's face flashed in her mind. The hand became slim and dark, the fingers long and thin. Jellied water swirled around the lily pads. Farah's voice broke through the narrow window at the back. Her great-aunt was praying. The water inched coolly up as Daisha sank; under the murk, her legs shrank and grew. She lifted her chin like a crocodile and waited for a sign to emerge.

*

In the morning, Daisha was instructed to clean the long-abandoned schoolroom at the end of the quad. It had no bed, only two chairs and an old desk. The desk drawer was empty apart from a stiffened alphabet primer. Daisha pushed her collection of stolen objects inside before starting to tidy. She opened the door again in case her great-aunt came by, but the quad was quiet. She was sweeping when Altair came in clutching his rucksack.

Only the cockerel was in the yard, so sleepy in the heat that it hadn't bothered announcing the visitor. I think great-aunt's having her nap, Daisha said.

I'll wait - I only need to tell her that your mother and aunts are coming next week, which is good news, isn't it? he said. He sat down next to the desk.

She waited for him to elaborate, but he didn't. The topic of her mother's illness made her nervous, anyway: as if, at some point, Daisha would have to claim responsibility if it got worse again.

Carry on with your tidying, he said. He reached into his bag and pulled out a newspaper. She moved stiffly, listening as he shifted about on the rickety chair. His eyes were shut when she turned again. Head tilted back, and he looked comfortable enough to fall asleep. His unshaven neck glistened in the heat. The collar of his loose green shirt fluttered in the breeze and exposed the V of his chest.

After a while, Daisha sat down on the other chair. She leant over to see if he really was asleep. The newspaper teetered on his thigh. The gap between his chest and shirt gaped so she could see where his skin became dark and wiry. His steady breath halted for a second and his lashes bristled as Daisha drew closer. He parted his lips, opened his eyes and he stared into hers for a few long seconds.

She dragged the chair along the ground as she moved away.

What are you doing? he asked, his voice soft and insistent.

I thought there was something wrong, she lied.

Did you? Why would something be wrong?

He was smiling as he spoke. She felt as if she had been caught at something, but she wasn't in trouble - in fact, she could have carried on.

She got up quickly when she heard a door unlocking. He didn't move. He only sat up in the chair, gave her a sidelong look. The cockerel blocked her path momentarily. It examined them both with sly, hooded eyes before trotting off at the sound of Farah in the quad.

*

After dinner that evening, Daisha and Farah lay on the bed. That was their routine after Farah closed up the rest of the house - there was nowhere else for Daisha to go.

I was fifteen years old, Farah said over the ceiling fan. It spun muggy air above them. I left home to come here at that age. I watched a bride on a video film recently, and she didn't even cry. What's a wedding if the bride doesn't cry? On my wedding day, I cried and fainted and refused to get up off the floor. They had to beg me and then I fainted again. People spoke about it for years. Farah clawed the air, as if she were prising down her younger body.

I'm not old-fashioned, she said. She violently scratched the flaking heels that she had earlier made Daisha massage with Sudocrem. They were the bad days, she said. No one will marry an uneducated woman now. Your mother didn't teach our language to you - you use little baby words.

Daisha lay still to stop her sanitary pad rustling stickily up her crotch.

You don't have to think about marriage for a long

time, Farah said. Until you are 20 at least, very old. But life is still much easier in this country. And then there's your mother. There's no one here to make your life difficult. You've got people watching out for you, moyna.

*

Daisha had been there for three weeks now. Her secret walks became longer but she never seemed to lose sight of the house. It was a grey box on the flat land, with no other buildings nearby. No one ever appeared in the distance. Only Altair lived on the same side of the river and she would have had to enter the forest to find him. Sometimes she imagined him meeting her half-way.

But when his familiar figure headed towards the house one afternoon, she only panicked. She stumbled in the field's boggy patches in her haste to get to the veranda. Have you been exploring? he asked, without looking up. He was leaning against the rusty balustrade and hadn't knocked on the door. His shirt sleeves were rolled up so that she could see the thin hair on his arms.

You should see more of these fields, he said. All that green is good for your eyes. Maybe I'll take you myself - it's very safe.

In the city she and her aunts had been driven everywhere in rickshaws and she had been warned not to look at men going by in case she attracted attention. She wondered what it would be like to be aimless in the fields with Altair. She stood against the railing with him. She was afraid of taking out her key, in case he commented, but he didn't seem to be interested in going inside.

He reached into his bag and brought out a small bag of fruit. I gathered these this morning. They'll start rotting soon - they taste the best just before then, he said. He wrapped her hand around the bag handle.

Go ahead, he said, eat.

We can have carefree talks, can't we? he asked, as she took out a guava.

After I last saw you, God told me that you were suffering, he said.

What are you talking about? Daisha asked, her mouth full.

You don't ask about your mother. All the gossips about you in England. Your mother and your aunts tell me. They worry about you. I know these gossips are not true, of course, but no one else cares.

Daisha remembered the long phone calls, how he had arrived at the Sylhet townhouse shortly after they did and been ushered into another room with her aunts and mother.

The men and women in the town make things up about all the girls, she said.

They don't know what's inside. God told me that you have great potential for goodness.

He looked at her so sadly that she believed him. He placed his hands on her shoulders. His touch made her feel childish for running away in the schoolroom. She had to squint upwards to see him. She imagined herself glowing in the sunlight that swaddled the veranda.

Do you have something in your eye? he laughed. He lifted his hands and his outline bore down on her. She felt so alone that she no longer cared what she said.

I don't want to make mum feel worse.

Neither does anyone else. Now go inside so that your great-aunt doesn't notice that you're missing.

He took up his bag and she watched him disappear in the fringe of trees.

*

That evening, Daisha helped her great-aunt to the bedroom after her shower.

It was the other way around once, me lifting and carrying you from room to room, Farah said, after catching her breath.

Farah handed a plastic tortoiseshell comb to Daisha, who ran it through her great-aunt's damp yellow and white hair. She twisted a fistful into a bun and secured it with kirby grips retrieved from her own.

Altair sees so much good in you, I can tell from the effort he makes to visit. Is he teaching you how to pray?

He said he would, Daisha lied, without knowing why.

Your mother should have taught you to pray, but her illness makes her very neglectful. Never mind.

Why do people think he's so special? Daisha asked. Agreeing with her great-aunt's criticism made her uneasy, as if she was entering into a lonely pact.

He has a connection with God - do not question it. He is very good at talking to the young people, *wily* baadmash boys and girls from England especially. Although sometimes they even say that he goes too far with his claims.

What does he do?

He was so much more mysterious to her than she was to him, Daisha thought.

Don't question me so much! Farah said. She looked confused. He has a gift, that is what I know. What that gift is, I do not know. He is *modern*, I suppose. When he speaks, you should listen.

Farah took the tasbih from the bedpost and started counting the faceted beads with her knotty fingers.

He will keep you in his prayers. I will also pray for you, moyna.

Daisha watched her great-aunt fall asleep sitting up.

Being prayed for implied that she was beyond human help, Daisha thought. A prayer was a sticky web outside of which she couldn't survive.

*

The quad filled with the smell of boiling chicken on the day of the visit from Daisha's mother and aunts. Daisha threw water over a bloody patch of earth where, in the morning, the slaughtered hen had squirted blood from its neck before collapsing. The rooster watched Daisha as she refilled the bucket. Farah had spared the rooster because its short legs amused her.

Join me on the veranda! It is a beautiful day! her great-aunt shouted from the front of the house.

Daisha went and sat next to her looking out at the field. She ate from the bowl of wet chanachur hammocked between her legs. Farah kept her gaze trained on the trees in expectation, only shifting to angle her fan better.

The guests emerged out of the greenery one by one. Altair was behind her mother and her aunts carrying their handbags. Her great-aunt went to greet them, while Daisha waited for them to step up to the house.

Her mother looked different. Her hair had been pulled back, its fuzzy halo sleek. Her mother's newly youthful appearance was worrying, as if she could only become better when Daisha wasn't there. On the veranda, she curtained Daisha in the voluminous fabric of her sari.

Everything good? she said, tight-lipped, before retracting.

Her older aunt leaned forward to examine Daisha. Her eyes were sad above her lowered sunglasses. Daisha had thought that was because she had no children, but then she remembered how her mother said that she herself regretted having any. The younger aunt nodded approvingly. Nothing sticking out this time! she whispered, looking down at the airy salwar kameez that Daisha was wearing and the dainty little heels that stopped Daisha's trouser cuffs trailing the ground.

The guests all stood outside turning this way and that to look at the surroundings. Daisha watched Altair and her relatives speak as if they were reciting from a book in turns. She was not used to this delicate, polite version of Sylheti; she could only make out that Altair was promising that the bridge would return Sangupur to its former status. She was afraid of speaking to Altair in their shared English in case anyone noticed how they were together. And she could tell from the way he walked past her into the house that he didn't want to give away their connection either.

She waited in the reception while her great-aunt took them on a tour around the quad. Farah paused occasionally after a description of a long departed relative, like a tour guide anticipating questions. No one asked any. They only peered into each room briefly and adjusted their sunglasses or their shawls.

They came back to the narrow room and sat down opposite each other: Farah and her great-aunt lined on one bench and the guests and Altair on the other. They carried on talking for a long while as if Daisha wasn't there, until her great-aunt instructed her to bring another tray of betelnut. When she returned from the kitchen, wobbling on her heels, her aunts opened their mouths wide.

So clever, they said to Farah.

I've been teaching her everything. She's been a

great help. Obviously, you can see what a struggle it is for me with this stick. It will be very hard for me when you take her back, Farah said.

What's a few more weeks here? Altair said, suddenly. He spoke to her aunts and mother.

Yes, Farah said. Especially with Altair here to check on her.

Well, her mother said. She didn't carry on. When she went to pick up the nutcracker with a shaky hand, her sister took it over and chopped the betelnut for her.

What's a few more weeks? her younger aunt echoed. We haven't seen our sister for over ten years.

Daisha cleared her throat. She spoke quickly to avoid hearing her own imprecision.

But don't you want me to stay with you in town?

Her mother's gaze receded. Daisha knew that direct appeals made her nervous.

It is good to see where you're from, her aunts said. Some girls, they hardly ever come back, and forget everything.

The girl is learning a great deal here. Her prayers and more about the culture, Altair said.

I knew that I could rely on you, Daisha's mother, turning to him. It is lonely in England. Girls can bring a unique shame. My sisters said that you would be helpful.

You're very lucky, her aunt said. He doesn't just speak to any family.

Although Altair was many years younger than Daisha's mother, she looked as if he had come to rescue her.

Daisha is a good girl, he said.

I know she has people to look out for her here, Daisha's mother said.

The more there was of other people, the less there

needed to be of her mother, Daisha realised.

*

Daisha sat by herself in the old schoolroom. It had been a week since the visitors came; now monsoon season had begun. In between storms that hammered the rooftop, the house was silent. She twisted the radio dial to the English language station. The pop song now sounded childish compared with the gentle plucked strings and high-pitched singing she heard on the other stations. The difference in how the music sounded made her feel travel-sick - when the outside changed, and the inside remained the same. Or maybe she meant homesick if the sickness came from home becoming unfamiliar in the distance. She switched the radio off and went to find her great-aunt whose talking would at least occupy her until she fell asleep.

*

Altair visited the following week. He arrived again shortly before they ate. Daisha set the table as he talked to Farah from the bedroom doorway about a meeting he'd been to in the city. He peered down at the steaming dishes of fish and vegetables. Daisha put down an extra plate before he spoke. I must leave soon, he said, while seating himself.

The bridge is coming along – I've had meetings with many officials now, Altair said as they ate. They said a road must be decided on first, Altair said. And then we can draw up the bridge plans.

They'll have to carry my dead body across it at this rate, Farah said.

Altair poured water for a little too long and it splashed onto the table.

Outside, there was the long high whirring noise

that came before a storm. A warm breeze drifted into the room.

Daisha, Altair said, turning away. The bridge will be here by the time that you come back. No more journeys on the boat.

She nodded because she didn't want to embarrass him any further. His life outside of Sangupur was probably unimaginable to someone like Farah. He smiled at her almost subliminally. In the half-light, his smooth skin gleamed and his features softened. She couldn't hold both ideas of him at once.

The room whitened with lightning before she could reply. Within minutes, the earth in the quad was cratering and churning under pelting rain. They had finished eating but no one got up to clear the table.

I can still go home, he said, without moving.

You can't leave now, Farah said, following his gaze into the quad. What will people say if I send you out in this tufaan? Daisha, take him to one of the spare rooms. He can sleep there tonight.

She theatrically removed one of the keys tied to her waist and handed it over to Daisha along with a Hurricane lamp from the sideboard.

Make sure he's comfortable. How will I feel if he's uncomfortable? she said.

*

Daisha opened the door and set the lamp down on the dresser. It illuminated a large bed. A single chair had been placed near the door for the sitter to catch a breeze. She unlocked the almirah in the corner and retrieved some fresh-smelling linen; it was washed regularly for guests who never came. Altair took the set from her arms. You don't have to go now, he said, when he finished making the bed.

She sat on the edge of the chair, letting the rain from the open door splatter her ankles and feet. Outside, drops bounced mid-air like a torn hem. Daisha half-listened out for Farah's sandals slapping on the wet concrete, but it was impossible to make out anything under the downpour.

I should leave, she said, hoping that he would tell her otherwise.

Are you afraid of this weather? he asked.

He was now sitting on the bed opposite her.

No - I'm used to it now, she said.

So why are you always in a rush?

I'm not, she said. There's nowhere to go.

You aren't so different, he said.

From who? she asked.

Other girls who come here.

Daisha waited for him to describe how they spoke, whether he thought they were pretty. She didn't want to hear and yet she needed to know.

I was close to some of those girls, he carried on. They could tell me how they felt. One even lay next to me sometimes and we fell asleep together without doing anything.

He touched his unshaven chin.

How old was the girl? Daisha asked.

A little bit older than you, he said.

Daisha stared down at her sandals, which her older aunt had bought in the market for her. Their pink bobbles shone in the dark.

Where did you do that? she asked.

At her parents' house.

The rain had stopped now. His voice was steady against the silence, the background dulled as in a phone call.

The bed is comfortable for two people, he said.

You don't have to go back out there. We could lie here for a while until we both go to sleep. Soon I'll be too busy to come around as often.

He lifted the bed cover and stared down at it and back up at her.

No one has ever asked you this before? he said.

Daisha didn't know anyone her own age who had ever done it in a bed, unless it was the middle of the day and their parents were out. She felt a dull pressure between her legs. She wanted to leave the room and breathe in deeply before coming back. But she didn't want to stop him talking.

What are you feeling? he asked.

What do you mean?

About staying here with me, he said.

Nothing, she said.

Those are normal feelings, he said. What you feel in your body towards me. Wanting to stay here.

He looked at her urgently and widened his eyes as if to say that he understood - he really did. She could tell him anything.

There was nothing she could keep from him, she thought. She would never know him unless she said yes to staying.

I can sleep here, she said.

He slapped a hand down on the wooden bedframe so hard that it startled her.

You cannot act on those body feelings with another person. Otherwise, God will punish you, he said.

His voice rose and filled the room.

He didn't mean only himself, but any other man, Daisha realised.

It's here. Can you see it? he asked.

What? Daisha pressed one foot firmly onto the

ground.

The darkness. Your desire. I've drawn it out, he said.

She opened her mouth to laugh but he got up and walked towards her.

He kneeled on the floor.

He was careful not to brush against her knees or her legs or chest as he reached forward. The crooked white line of his parting glowed in the dark.

I can save you from yourself, he said.

His shaking hand grappled with her head, stilled it. Fingers tightened around her skull.

See - I've brought the desire out of you, so you don't have to act on it.

He tightly ringed her wrist and placed her lowered hand on his face.

I'm giving you a gift - you can do the same for another person, he said. *This* is how you can touch someone.

When she finally left the room, there only remained the pressure of his forehead against her palm, the wetness of his tears on her fingers.

*

Farah's bedroom door was closed but not locked yet. She was lying on top of the sheets fanning herself.

You were talking a long time, she said.

Maybe you should have sat with us, Daisha replied. She gathered her bedclothes. Her balance steadied as she made her way to the small bathroom.

You only have a few more days here - I don't want to get in the way.

Farah carried on talking as Daisha shut the door behind her.

We could walk to your great-uncle's grave

tomorrow. You haven't been in the fields yet. After that I will be alone. Altair will not come, no one will come. I could have got married again and gone somewhere else, but I said no. Once was enough.

The bed always transported Farah to the past. After a certain time in the evening, she stayed there.

The shutters were still open in the bathroom, which was bright with moonlight. The garbage heap smell pulsed through the window. She sat down on the cool plastic seat of the toilet, tensed her bare feet against the rough floor as she peed.

A rusty sliding lock sounded from further down the quad. Altair. She half-expected to hear him moving about, but there was nothing. Only her great-aunt snoring.

Daisha released a long, jagged breath after she got up. Her moon-lit face flashed in the smeared glass above the basin. She had forgotten to turn on the light. Sometimes, after returning, she would see that same reflection trapped in the glass. Years later, when she was more than twice as old, its occasional appearance became reassuring. She changed her clothes. The mirror blackened as the moon slid under again.

Farah called out in her sleep: who is it? Still me, Daisha said as she joined her in bed.

Notes on Contributors

David Butler's most recent short story collection is Fugitive (Arlen House, 2021). His novel City of Dis (New Island) was shortlisted for the Kerry Group Irish Novel of the Year, 2015.

Helen Harjak was born in Estonia, studied literature and philosophy in Scotland, and now lives in London, where she works as a freelance journalist and copy-editor. Her fiction has been published in Okay Donkey, Visual Verse, Fudoki Magazine, and Small Good Things, an anthology by Dahlia Books.

Catherine McNamara grew up in Sydney, ran away to Paris to write and ended up in West Africa co-running a bar. Love Stories for Hectic People won Best Short Story Collection in the Saboteur Awards 2021. The Cartography of Others was finalist in the People's Book Prize. Catherine lives in Italy and her stories have been published widely.

Andy Mead is a retired teacher who was brought up in Jamaica in the 1960's and still retains strong links with that island he still regards as home. He has an MA in creative writing from the University of Chichester and is now a private tutor, writer and storyteller.

Jackie Morris is a recent graduate of The Open University's MA in Creative Writing (2021). She writes short form and flash fiction and spends far too much time on Twitter. Her husband has no interest in chickens.

Peter Newall was born in Sydney, Australia, where he worked variously in a naval dockyard, as a musician and as a lawyer, but has since lived in Kyoto, Japan, and now in Odessa, Ukraine, where he sings for a popular local r'n'b group, the Newall Band. He has been published in England, Hong Kong, Australia and the USA.

Diana Powell's stories have featured in a number of competitions, including the 2020 SoA ALCS Tom-Gallon Award (runner-up) and the 2019 ChipLit Prize (winner). They have also been published in several anthologies and journals, such as 'Best (British) Short Stories 2020'. Her novella, 'Esther Bligh', was published in 2018 by Holland House Books. Her collection, 'Trouble Crossing the Bridge' came out in 2020. Her novella, 'The Sisters of Cynvael', won the 2021 Cinnamon Press Literature Award, and will be published next year.

Anju Sharma grew up in Uttar Pradesh, India, majored in history from Delhi University, worked as a copy-writer, taught copywriting, then went back to being a student – this time of literature – purely through the act of intense reading. Her writing has appeared or is forthcoming in The Maine Review, The Margins, The Forge and Nelle. She is shortlisted for Bridport Short Story Prize 2022 and longlisted for Desperate Literature Short Fiction prize 2022. She is presently working on a novel.

Lui Sit writes in multiple genres including adult short fiction, memoir and children's middle grade books. She is an alumnus of several writers' development schemes including A Brief Pause, London Writers Award and

Penguin WriteNow. Her stories are published in journals and anthologies including MAINSTREAM, Superlative, Short Good Things, Fudoki, City of Stories and Out of The Box.

Zakia Uddin is a short story writer whose previous work has been published by The White Review, The Stinging Fly and Granta. She lives in London.

About the Judge

Jarred McGinnis was chosen by the Guardian as one of the UK's ten best emerging writers. His debut novel 'The Coward' was selected for BBC 2's Between the Covers, BBC Radio 2's Book Club and listed for the Barbellion Prize.

His short fiction has been commissioned for BBC Radio 4 and appeared in respected journals in the UK, Canada, USA and Ireland. He is or has been an Associate Writer for Spread the Word, a mentor for the Word Factory, a fellow of the London Library's T S Eliot Emerging Writer Programme and a Writer-in-Residence for First Story.

He also has a PhD in Artificial Intelligence, but mostly he inspires the able-bodied by using public transport and taking his daughters to the playground.

Writers write. Actors read.
Audience listens. Everybody wins.

Established in 2007, Liars' League is an award-winning bimonthly fiction night, where professional actors perform brand-new short stories by writers from around the world. Our readings have been broadcast on BBC Radio 4, and our ever-growing online archive holds over 700 stories (and counting) – all available to watch, read and listen to for free.

Events are held on the second Tuesday of every second month in central London, at The Phoenix pub (38 Cavendish Square, W1G 0PP). Performances are filmed for YouTube, and podcast for free download.

If you like the sound of what we do and want to join our mailing list for information on our regular events and themed deadlines, email **liars@liarsleague.com** with Mailing List in the subject line. If you'd like to submit or perform a story, please visit our website, **www.liarsleague.com**.

Twitter/Instagram: @liarsleague
YouTube: www.youtube.com/liarsleague
Facebook: www.facebook.com/liarsleague

Director: Katy Darby. Regular host: Liam Hogan.